THE
PASSENGER

THE
Passenger

Maryam Sachs

Translated by
GAEL SCHMIDT-CLEACH

QUARTET

First published in 2013 by
Quartet Books Limited
A member of the Namara Group
27 Goodge Street, London W1T 2LD

A catalogue record for this book
is available from the British Library

ISBN   978 0 7043 7316 7

Typeset by Antony Gray
Printed and bound in Great Britain by
T J International Ltd, Padstow, Cornwall

I dedicate this book to

PHILIPP, FREDERIK AND ROYA

ACKNOWLEDGEMENTS

My special thanks to Naim Attallah whose vision
I have always admired, Gaël Schmidt-Cléach who
is a unique translator, Cyrielle Ayakatsikas for
her brilliant editing in French, Anna Stothard
for her support from the beginning to the end,
Christopher Lebrun whose painting 'Lift' has
lifted the book to another level, Wilfried Dickhoff
who is the most accomplished graphic designer
for all my books and Giancarlo Cattaneo for the
spontaneous portrait.

There is no such thing as an empty space or an empty time.
There is always something to see, something to hear.
In fact, try as we may to make a silence, we cannot.

John Cage

Silence, Music, Silent Music

6:34 pm

There's a long line of cabs just outside the airport. I jump into the first one, glad I won't have to wait, and sink into the back seat. The black leather is still warm from the day's heat. The front passenger seat, folded forward to leave customers room to stretch their legs out, is buried under a pile of books, bags, and water bottles. I start emptying my own bag on the seat next to me. I don't travel light; it's always full of books, newspapers, and other knick-knacks. Most of the time I actually have to carry two bags around.

The car smells of cherry-flavoured chewing gum. It's not the most pleasant smell, but at least the radio isn't on. I didn't get any sleep on the plane and my head is killing me, I don't know if I could have dealt with the inane babble of French radio. Actually, I could use a couple of aspirins before we get going, to help me relax before the party tonight.

'Where are we going?'

'Sorry,' I say, snapping out of my reverie. '280, Boulevard Raspail, please.'

I've made the trip so many times: I know it should take about an hour to get there, maybe a little longer if there's traffic. My friend Dino hates travelling for work, and I can relate. I always tell myself I'll use this time to read, or respond to emails, or even make to-do lists, but it never works out that way. Maybe there are people who manage to get work done in these conditions, but I just can't. I'm easily distracted and overwhelmed by even the tiniest event or change, so end up wasting huge amounts of time being wholly unproductive.

Inside the taxi the air is damp. I roll down the window.

My son is turning twenty-one today. It's a pretty big deal for him. I remember how exhilarating it felt when I turned twenty-one, when I became, finally, an adult. I was still living in East Berlin at the time, and studying at the Humboldt University. I still remember that year vividly as a time of courage and innovation.

I lived in a tiny studio, on the top floor of an abandoned building, right in the middle of East Berlin: 31 Marienburger Strasse. I'd moved in on my twenty-first birthday. I didn't pay rent – there was no one to pay rent to. My one and only neighbour was an old lady who lived on the ground floor. The city had plans to renovate deserted buildings such as that one, but no one felt like evicting the few people still living there. The law was powerless against our sense of community; as long as there were people living in these flats, no one would even try to tear them down.

Even though my new 17-square-metre flat was much bigger than the dilapidated student room I'd just left, it still felt too small for me, and soon I had plans for an extension. Soon after the move into my new apartment, I decided to tear down the wall between my flat and the adjoining one. I spent the next three nights digging through 70 centimetres of concrete. Nothing is impossible. It was hard work, and exhausting, but I needed more space, and that was the only way I was going to get it.

Next I had to furnish my new home. In the streets lay windows and furniture meant for urban renewal projects that would never come to pass, so like everyone else, I just grabbed what I needed. We were all in it together, back then; if someone from the neighbourhood came looking for help, you helped them. I was no good with the technical stuff, but some friends did the electrical wiring for me, and a month later I had my own fully habitable 30-square-metre apartment.

My daughter Elinor is in charge of the birthday party. I picture her placing flowers in small vases that she'll then arrange on the tables. The rooms in our apartment on Boulevard Raspail are very bright, not at all like those in my old Berlin flat. There's very little furniture: my husband Martín and I like our space. For tonight's dinner we put three tables in the middle of the living room. On the walls are mostly photographs, as well as portraits by Joseph Beuys, whom I consider the quintessential contemporary German artist. We own a few of his ready-mades as well.

Things must be well under way there. The cook has probably been at work all day, making sauces, cooking lamb, veal, and duck. Just thinking of the upcoming feast is enough to make me salivate.

6:37 pm

I've barely spared a look for the driver since we left the airport. I did notice his deep voice when he asked where I was going, though.

We're driving along the same route I always take when leaving the airport. We leave the trucking company buildings that border the highway behind, and soon I can see the 'Paris–Centre' sign that hangs from the flyover.

The air I breathe through the open window carries the unmistakable smell of Parisian pollution. The walls of the tunnel are covered in colourful graffiti, and I wish I could take a piece of them back with me, as a gift to Lukas. My son loves street art, but I know that what he'd really want is a piece of the Berlin Wall. The graffiti on it is a reminder of upheaval and great heartbreak. Amid the thousands of signatures and dates, you'll find portraits of some of history's greatest revolutionary figures as well as messages of universal love and peace. Some of those are like short poems. 'Tear down this wall and all the others will follow' is one I remember; 'Love is stronger than concrete' is another, and 'Will the Wall disappear in the fog of history?' a third one. I'd love to get my son a piece of the Wall inscribed with one of those messages.

This year, though, I'm giving him two old coins bearing the effigy of Alexander the Great that I found in Greece. For as long as I can remember he has been fascinated by Alexander; as a child, he made us watch countless films about his life and time. He is now studying history, and I wouldn't be surprised if he were to pursue a career in academia, teaching ancient history.

I had the coins made into cufflinks for my son. I was thrilled when I came across them in an old antique shop in Athens. To me they are not only coins or cufflinks, they're also a symbol, a message. They are an emblem of Alexander's relentless conquering spirit and his fascination with Persian traditions. They actually remind me of when Lukas was a child and I read him stories about History's greatest conquerors before he went to bed. Those made such an impact on him that fifteen years later, he still remembers them. They were stories about will, courage, devotion, strength, intelligence, and sensitivity, and that's what comes to mind when I look at this gift, too. In the box I put a card with a quote by Alexander: 'There is nothing impossible to him who will try.'

I am beginning to doze off when I hear a voice that seems to come from far away. 'I usually stay home when it's too hot,' the driver says. 'My colleagues don't care, but I can't stand the heat.'

I don't really know what to make of this comment. I mutter some sort of response while looking at his profile in the rear-view mirror. He sounds somewhat foreign, Middle Eastern maybe. Or southern European. Not Greek, though. I just got back from there, and I still have the lovely accent ringing in my ears.

He's about my age, with long brown hair and a light beard. The sleeves of his blue polo shirt are rolled up, revealing complex networks of veins on his arms and hands. He drives in an easy, fluid way, all the while chewing his cherry-flavoured gum. He sometimes reaches up to touch his Bluetooth earpiece or push his wireframe glasses back up on his nose, but otherwise his calloused hands never leave the wheel.

The road morphs into a three-lane highway as it gets closer to Paris. Soon I can see the sign for the Porte de la Chapelle exit. I've taken the Périphérique so many times, I could navigate it almost by ear. Here's Porte de la Chapelle, then Porte de Clignancourt. A little further down is Porte d'Asnières, then Porte Maillot. On the left side of the highway are housing projects, tall buildings whose roofs are covered by billboards selling everything from television sets to insurance. It seems every time I drive into the city I can't help but stare at them as I pass them by.

6:38 pm

I could strike up a conversation with the driver – he seems willing enough – but I'd rather let my mind wander back to Greece and to the blue waves of the Mediterranean, whose slow undulations sculpt the horizon. The line between the calm sea and the cloudless sky is almost invisible, the transition from one shade of blue to the next almost imperceptible. It always reminds me of the delicate shadows of Sugimoto's black-and-white seascapes, with their fragile, sometimes disconcerting lines. A thin grey line stands for the huge chasm between the sea and the sky, which never touch. Or if they do it is only in my mind. I love how it makes me feel as if I were untethered and adrift. I can't believe it was only a few hours ago that I was looking at that landscape.

We never think about the effect departures can have, our own or someone else's. It's like taking a pair of scissors to a piece of paper. We suffer many such cuts over our lifetime, deep and superficial, and at the end of the day they help us remember what happened, and why.

When the man I loved left me there was no why, though. One day he just disappeared without a trace, without a note. I wonder, did he feel the same cut I did?

I was born in 1964 in Tübingen, in West Germany. My father was an engineer, my mother a history teacher who wrote poetry during her spare time. That was her way of breaking free from the routine of her life.

Everything changed in 1968, when my father died in a car crash. I was four. My mother was from Leipzig, and after my father's death, she decided to go back to whatever family she still had there. So we found ourselves moving back to East Germany just as half the population was trying to cross the border in the other direction. After 1949, anyone leaving East Germany permanently was either a refugee or an illegal immigrant. Movement from one state to the other was closely monitored, and whenever we wished to visit even family members in the West we had to fill out pages and pages of forms and provide detailed information about our relatives. Similarly, West Germans could only visit East Germany if they obeyed a number of restrictions, and could only stay for a very short time. Despite all that, relatives sometimes came to visit for a few days.

My mother did all she could for us to be allowed to stay in East Germany. We first moved to Leipzig, shortly after my father's death, under the pretence of visiting my grandparents. At first glance it looked like we would not be staying long; after all, we'd only packed two suitcases. But my mother had already decided to stay and to apply for a residence permit. That apparently spontaneous decision made no sense to the East German communist officials, who ordered an investigation into my mother's motivations. Not that there were any: my mother simply didn't feel strong enough to raise me alone and far from her family.

They confiscated her passport and interned her in a transit camp, on the banks of the Elbe River. They then started looking into her past, checking whether she had ever been affiliated with any political or criminal organisation, had ever been linked to an intelligence agency. Every day two buses would stop in front of the camp, one going west, the other east, and a guard would call out names and orient people towards one of the buses. You were never told which bus you were going to board in advance, or even exactly when your name would be called.

After five months of waiting, my mother was finally allowed to remain in East Germany. Meanwhile I had been staying at my grandparents', people I barely knew and who had never shown me much affection. Soon after my mother was released we moved to Berlin, where we met up with my uncle, who'd married a Berliner before the Wall was built.

I had an ordinary childhood, and never felt like being raised in East Germany put me at a disadvantage. Culture played a central role in my upbringing; my father's love for the opera was passed down to me thanks in large part to my uncle, who often took me to the Berliner Staatsoper. I still remember the first time we went: I was twelve and he took me to see Offenbach's *The Tales of Hoffmann*, a favourite of my father's.

As a young adult I kept going regularly to the opera, buying five-mark tickets with my friends for the cheapest seats, way up on the balcony. I was twenty-one when I fell in love with a tenor, a Wagner specialist whose voice had entranced me. He stepped on stage like a god out of the darkness and his voice washed over me in a wave of intense happiness. The power of his voice was such that it blinded me, and in the darkness his words were like arrows aimed straight at my heart.

My friend must have thought I had fallen asleep, and she nudged me gently with her elbow. I jumped and sat up straight to show her I hadn't dozed off. Truth be told, I felt like I was dreaming. His confidence, his presence enthralled me. He sang *Lohengrin* in a voice at once deep and warm that I can still hear all those years later.

He was the greatest tenor I'd ever heard. Every note he sang made my heart burst with joy, and my knees trembled every time I laid eyes on him. He was twenty years older than I was, and our tempestuous relationship began most abruptly and unexpectedly when we ran into each other in a bar after one of his performances. My friends had badgered me to go with them, and I had reluctantly agreed. He was standing at the counter with his back to us, but I recognised him immediately, of course. Without thinking I rushed over to the bar under the pretence of ordering drinks for everyone. We were so violently drawn to each other that even later we couldn't understand what had happened to us. Even today I cannot explain it.

In the summer of 1985 I became pregnant. The idea of carrying the child of the man I loved and admired made me happier than I'd ever been before, and he, too, was ecstatic when I told him the news. It didn't last, though, and soon joy gave way to confusion and distress. I was much too young and inexperienced, not ready at all to be a mother. All of a sudden I had to act like an adult with responsibilities, and it didn't take me long to understand that I could never keep that child. After all, what future did the two of us have together? Then there was my mother. I knew how much she'd suffered from having to raise me on her own after my father's death. If I'd had a child so young, it would have caused her yet more pain. She could never have brought herself to trust the man I loved, would have remained always convinced that he would eventually leave me – and she wouldn't have been wrong. She would never have understood.

So I made the most difficult choice of my life. By the

time I finally got an abortion two weeks later, I was acutely aware of my own pregnancy. I felt nauseous every morning, then ravenous for the rest of the day. I could feel life growing inside me, which caused long bouts of introspection during which I discovered things about myself I'd never suspected. I barely slept and, sleepless night after sleepless night, the circles under my eyes grew darker and darker. I felt exposed and vulnerable, true, but also certain I was doing the right thing. Eventually sadness gave way to determination. What hurt the most, was my tenor's reaction when I told him what I had decided. 'This is unfair,' he snapped. 'You're not the only one to have a say in this.' I couldn't believe just how selfish he was being, I was both surprised and disappointed. Not long after that, he was gone and I was alone. I'd lost both my child and the man I loved. His friends told me he had fled East Germany. No one has heard from him since. I never saw him again.

Maybe he was right to have left me. Maybe I deserved it, I don't know. But that wound has remained open, because I've never let myself look back on what happened, not really. Regardless of how much pain this may have caused me, or may cause me still, all these years later, I've never been able to face the reality of it. Denial won't bring you peace, though. I know this is a part of me that I will have no choice but to face some day, if I ever want to leave the pain behind and become a new person.

I wrote him I don't know how many letters – farewell letters, letters that betrayed my distress and my inability to move on or fill the void he'd left behind him. I never sent any of them. Even in those unsent letters, I never asked him why he left, or what he thought of what had happened. It was too late to think about all that. I've kept those questions buried deep within me, knowing full well that they would inevitably resurface one day.

Sometimes one simple event is all it takes for things to fall apart. An accident can herald a beginning – or an ending. Losing a loved one might be the most painful thing we ever have to deal with, but when that happens, we know it is only a beginning, that many other such losses will follow.

6:40 pm

The sky is a striking shade of dark blue, I just have to take a picture. I take my camera out of my purse. There can't be much battery left. In fact, I took so many pictures in Greece that there hardly any memory left, either.

The sky has already started changing colour, you can clearly see the outlines of the buildings. Soon this magic moment will be over.

'I'm glad you'd rather be taking pictures than complaining about the traffic!'

Has the driver directly addressed me since we left the airport?

'Are you being sarcastic?'

'Not at all!' he says. 'If we all just knew how to always find the silver lining, life would be much nicer.'

I don't know what to make of this compliment.

I stash my camera back into my purse. I'll have to remember to charge it before the party, so that it lasts all night. I wanted to take a picture of the driver in the rearview mirror, but decided against it.

My phone starts ringing, but by the time I find it on the backseat next to me, it's stopped. This keeps happening to me. The call was from Martín. I try calling him back, but all I get is a busy signal.

Did I tell Elinor which vases I wanted her to use for the bouquets? Our silver cups should be fine. Before I left for Greece, I ordered an assortment of white and blue hyacinths, although it is not the season, to go with the blue tablecloths. I've discovered I like being in charge of the flat's decoration, which came as something of a surprise since I never cared about such details when I was younger. Fresh flowers were something we never had, back in East Germany. My mother wasn't big on aesthetic considerations.

My headache is subsiding, and I suddenly feel like sharing a moment with this stranger that is driving me home. There are so many questions I could ask him, like where he's from, or how he ended up here. Does he have another job? How did he become a Parisian cab driver, and what did he mean when he said he only drives when it's not too hot? Does he have a family?

Last summer I read *Night Roads*, a book written by a Russian expat working as a cab driver in Paris. He relates his experiences in a fresh and original way, and I was

19

struck by the subtlety with which he talks about all the people he met. 'Feelings are the only subject you know something about,' he writes, and I can't get that sentence out of my head.

Now I regret not saying anything back when the driver spoke to me. I wish I could find something to talk about, but I'm drawing a blank.

6:46 pm

Traffic is extremely dense on the Périphérique, especially considering it's the middle of August. The city seems to slow to a crawl in August, even to stop altogether at times. Paris can feel like a ghost town.

On my left, the Stade de France appears out of nowhere, like a giant flying saucer. I really need to talk to someone. I try calling my daughter, but it goes straight to voicemail.

'Hello darling,' I say. 'I'm on my way, I'll be there soon. Love.'

The driver must have sensed how tense I am. 'Don't worry,' he says, turning towards me, 'it'll be fine. Traffic should ease up as soon as we get to the centre. Shouldn't take more than forty-five minutes.'

'Thanks.'

His deep voice and accent are definitely intriguing, but I'm once again at a loss for words.

6:49 pm

An unexpected chiming noise, and I jump in surprise. Nothing but my phone telling me I just got an email. I don't feel like reading it right now. The silence in the taxi is starting to feel oppressive.

6:50 pm

My driver's phone starts ringing. Thank goodness for small favours! He soon cuts the conversation short, though, then turns to me and looks me straight in the eye.

'My mother is always worrying about me,' he says.

This time I'm not going to let this opportunity pass.

'How come you speak such good French?' I ask. I don't think my question is going to bother him, given that I myself have an accent that betrays my German origins. I still can't quite place his, though, and it makes me curious.

'I'm from Romania, and I learned French in school. Everyone speaks several languages, there. Romanian, of course, but also French, Italian, German, Russian, even Hungarian.' He sounds very friendly and cheerful, which surprises me a little.

'Does your mother still live there?'

'Yes. I usually drive there twice a year to visit my parents. Since leaving my country, I've lived pretty much everywhere. In France, in Canada … '

'Where in Canada?'

'I lived in Montreal for two years. I couldn't stand the cold, though, so I moved again.'

'Where to?'

'Japan.'

6:51 pm

Our conversation stops as quickly as it began, but I feel more relaxed now that we've exchanged a few words.

I realised that since I got into the cab, I've been thinking about anything and everything except about what I need to do before tonight's party. I really should make a list. Let's see, we need more wine glasses. I'll ask the neighbours if we can borrow a few.

I grab my notepad and find a pen hiding at the bottom of my bag. So, let's see:

> Matches
> Napkins
> Snacks
> Chocolate
> Scented candles

Paris really feels like home, now. I lead a quiet life with my family and my close friends – most of them expats like me. Even if I never directly suffered from it, I was always aware of just how cold and tough life in East Germany could be, and it taught me to really appreciate life and adapt to all kinds of circumstances. When Martín was transferred to the Institut Pasteur in Paris, I too saw it as a sort of new challenge and embraced our new life.

We're still on the Périphérique, just past Porte de Saint-Ouen. Back when we first moved to Paris and needed furniture and tableware, I used to go to the flea market there all the time. I loved to just walk around and browse. I picked up more than a few antiques for next to nothing.

My phone rings, and Martín's number appears on the screen. Speak of the devil.

'We're driving right by the flea market, Marché aux Puces. We really should go back one of these days. (...) Yeah, I tried calling back, but the line was busy. Are you already onboard the plane? When are you getting here? (...) They shouldn't arrive before eight thirty, if you're not there yet we'll just have to start without you. (...) OK see you then.'

6:54 pm

I hadn't noticed that my normally ankle-length skirt has ridden almost all the way up to my thighs. It must have happened when I moved around to find a more comfortable position. It looks almost like a mini-skirt now. How long has it been like that?

I don't want to make any sudden movement and draw the driver's attention. I wonder if he's noticed anything.

I usually refuse to show my legs, even when I'm tanned. My mother used to tell me I had ugly legs and that I must wear slacks or long skirts, and I've followed her advice in that matter ever since I was a teenager.

I'm squirming in my seat, trying to get my skirt back down. If the driver turns around and looks at me now, I might just die of embarrassment.

As if on cue, the car stops at a red light, and he turns to me. I can feel the heat in my cheeks.

'Is it just me, or is it really hot all of a sudden?' I say nervously.

'You're right, the air's really hot. Doesn't happen that often here, but it's very humid and hot tonight. It almost feels like a tropical jungle in here.'

'I hope it isn't going to rain.'

'From what I've heard, not until tomorrow morning, no.'

Great. At least that way those who want to smoke tonight will be able to do it on the balcony. Even though I smoke like a chimney, I hate it when my apartment smells like cold cigarette smoke after a party.

While putting my skirt back in place, I notice that the skin of my legs is very dry. I look like a crocodile! I really need to buy some skin cream. One more item to add to my grocery list!

'It can't have been easy leaving your country, can it?' I ask the driver, trying to start our conversation again.

'No, of course not. But in my family, we've never taken things lying down. My grandfather left for the United States before the Russians invaded. I don't know much about him; I tried finding out more, but no one would speak about it. My grandmother, on the other hand, stayed in Romania until after the soviets left. She just changed her name. Her husband's name was Schwarz, but her maiden name was Kiss, so she was never deported to Russia.'

'What a lovely name! I'm not surprised it saved her. So, do you share your grandmother's name?'

'Yes.'

'If I had to change my name, I think I'd pick yours. I mean it.'

He smiles for the first time, and our eyes meet in the rear-view mirror. It's like an invisible thread had just appeared between us.

I try to picture the Romanian flag. As a child, I used to know most countries' flags by heart, but I have to admit I've forgotten most of them.

'What colours?'

'Sorry?'

'Sorry, I was thinking aloud, trying to remember what the Romanian flag looks like.'

'It's got three vertical stripes. Cobalt blue, chrome yellow, vermilion red.'

Water, skin, blood. That's how I used to remember the colours on a flag.

Mr Kiss picks up where he left off.

'The living conditions in Romania were harsh. It gets very cold in the winter there, and we had few warm clothes. Food was rationed, too.

'When you live in an authoritarian country ruled through manipulation and deception, you can't help but dream of the freedom you hear is an inalienable right in democratic countries. Leaving Romania was never an easy decision to make, though, and my being an only child made it even harder. I didn't want to leave my parents behind, but in the end, they're the ones who convinced me to try to make it out of there, regardless of the risk. I wanted to become an artist, and I knew I couldn't do that there. All I had to lose by trying to escape, after all, was my life! I left the country in 1987, and two years later, the communist regime was finally falling. The new system wasn't any kinder to Romania, though, and my country went through a phase of instability and unrest, so I'm doubly happy I managed to make it out of there when I did. I still keep in touch with my family, though, and I visit them as often as I can.'

'Why did you come to Paris?'

'A lot of foreigners used to come to Romania on vacation, and among them were a French couple and their children, a thirteen-year-old girl and a sixteen-year-old boy. Back then, I worked part-time as a lifeguard. One day I was at my usual post on the beach when I noticed something strange going on in the water. No one had noticed the French girl drowning, and I rushed to save her. From that day on they considered me part of the family.'

He pauses, as if to remember their exact words. 'Please,' he says, 'Promise us that if you ever need something, anything at all, you'll get in touch with us.'

Then he sighs, and says, 'They gave me their address and phone number. When, five years later, I decided to try my luck and to leave Romania, they kept their promise. They took me in and told me I could stay for as long as I needed. They were so nice and generous, it was hard to believe.

'Not long after I got here, looking for a job, I got in

touch with some Romanian friends I knew had fled to France, too. That's how I started working as a cab driver for the first time. Meanwhile, I started dating Sophie, the girl I'd saved years before, and who was now eighteen. It didn't last, but we're still very good friends. I see them often.'

He seems lost in thought for a moment.

'You know, it's hard to feel safe when you're a refugee, even if you have a work permit.'

'Wait, you mean you could still get deported?'

'Absolutely. I know this family, they came here looking for a new start, tried to become a part of the community. They were deported a first time but they came back, hoping that if they enrolled their children in Parisian schools, they would be allowed to stay. They couldn't find a place that would accept them, though. They tried moving to Blois, but the local government wouldn't let them.'

'They drove here?'

'Yes.'

'I guess they must have tried to find a place to stay pretty much everywhere in France, right?'

'Yeah, they drove for thousands of miles.'

'Do you know where they are now?'

'They went south, and finally got lucky in Cannes, of all places. Can you believe it?'

'What happened?'

'Well, first they moved into a squat in Grasse, but they had no running water and no power. Thankfully, someone from Education Without Borders came to their help.'

'Have you kept in touch with them?'

'Yes, we talk on the phone every couple months. They told me the man who helped them was like a guardian angel. Apparently he's very fond of them and their children. He says they showed a real desire to learn and adapt to their new life.'

'Are there a lot of Romanian expats in other countries beside France?'

'I guess the largest community must be in Spain. But it's hard there, they face deportation at a moment's notice. There are close to a million, maybe. Most live right outside Madrid, in the city of Coslada. People call it "the Little Bucharest".'

'Why is it harder for them there?'

'They came to Spain a few years ago, some even before Romania became part of the EU. Spain needed workers then, particularly construction workers. But thanks to the economic crisis and the high unemployment rate, the Spanish government has decided to pass new measures to deport those workers they originally welcomed there.'

'Good thing you didn't go to Spain, then!'

'I thought about it, actually, in case I hadn't been allowed to stay here. But I didn't have to, thanks to my adoptive family. I owe them pretty much everything.'

Mr Kiss's story touched me deeply. When your situation seems desperate, the only thing you can count on is the beauty of human relations and the kindness of others. Easy for me to say, when I lost all faith at such a young age. I don't know why exactly. Perhaps it was partly my fault. Just like my tenor, I gave up on our love without giving much of a fight. Perhaps I should have tried to find him after he left.

Time passes, of course, yet at every moment of our lives we're liable to run into a link to our past, something that will yank us out of the present and bring a flood of memories back. Today I just ran into one of those links, in the form of a Romanian taxi driver.

The contrast between my current life and my childhood as an East German raised by her widowed mother is beyond words. It's as if at some point in my life I'd crossed from one world to another entirely different one.

At some stage in our relationship, fascinated as I was by the voice that had pierced my heart, I asked my tenor to give me singing lessons. The warmth of his voice made me feel confident and filled me with creative energy. He was so kind as to be irresistible; the more I learned to control my singing, the less I was able to control my desire for him. Our passion fed off the vibrations of our vocal chords. When he left East Germany, I decided to stop singing, a decision I've never gone back on. I knew that I had been able to sing only because of the strength of what we felt for each other and, without those feelings, my voice lacked soul.

Even as I forbade myself to try to find him, I've always wondered if I would see him again one day.

6:59 pm

All of a sudden a police siren goes off somewhere behind us. I can't help but feel a little paranoid when I hear that sound these days. It takes me back to a recent encounter with the police, which took place as Martín and I were driving home last month. It must have been around eleven thirty, and I have to admit I'd had a few glasses of wine and hadn't eaten much. I was driving and the police stopped us for speeding, and they made me breathe into a breathalyser. As my blood alcohol content was too high, I was cuffed and driven to the police station at high speed with the siren blaring. Since then I've become somewhat allergic to that deafening sound.

'Have you ever been handcuffed?' I ask Mr Kiss contritely.

'No.'

'I have.'

Mr Kiss, though, does not pick up on this comment.

Every topic leads us to another, opening new hidden doors. It's a lot like a game of Lego: at first all you've got is a few pieces, then you add more, and more, until you find yourself with entire buildings – the stories of our lives.

Mr Kiss finally seems to react to my last comment.

'My escape from Romania was at once the scariest, most painful moment of my life and the happiest. I crossed the border into Hungary one night in January of 1987.'

I've heard many tragic stories back in East Germany, of course, but I don't think one can ever really understand the stories of those who have lived through war and exile if one hasn't had the same experience. Too many people died trying to flee East Germany.

Mr Kiss and I have one crucial thing in common, as we both used to live in countries that were part of the Eastern bloc. Only he had to risk his life getting out, though, as I left for the West only after the fall of the Berlin Wall.

7:01 pm

Porte de Clichy. I can see the sign through the open window and feel the light end-of-summer breeze blowing through my hair.

I have to figure out what I'll wear tonight. It's my son's twenty-first birthday after all! I'm leaning towards black slacks and a white blouse, with a wide belt and my turquoise earrings.

7:05 pm

We drive up the Porte d'Asnières exit ramp to reach the bridge crossing the Périphérique we just left behind. I seem to have checked out again. I really want to hear Mr Kiss's story about his escape from Romania, though. Could it be that I'm afraid that hearing his story might lead me to look back on mine? I'm not given an opportunity to reflect on this, as Mr Kiss, having entered the taxi lane after stopping at a red light, picks up his story right where he left off, occasionally turning to look at me directly rather than in the rear-view mirror.

'I remember there was a football game playing on the television. A cold, cold night in January. There were two border guards, but they were completely absorbed in the game. There was a light mist, adding to the general dimness. The guards' breath stank of alcohol, Schnapps I guess. The heady smell permeated the air of the sentry box. I was shivering, partly because of the cold, but mostly because I was terrified. I could feel the blood throbbing in my veins, though, and I knew nothing could stop me. I can't remember what I might have been thinking, or just how many prayers I said, but I was absolutely certain of one thing: that was it, I was ready, ready to risk my life to be free. I had no choice but to leave. I was twenty and desperate to find meaning in my life. I knew I was worth five hundred levas, dead or alive. That was how much border guards got for capturing someone trying to flee the country.

'A few of my friends managed to leave the country and come to Paris, like me, but others were killed while trying to cross the border. My childhood friend Grigore left Romania a year after I did, travelled four hundred kilometres hidden in a lorry. Then he swam across the Danube to reach a village in Yugoslavia. They shot at him while he swam, but he managed to get away. He was thrown into jail by the Yugoslavian authorities and he stayed there for three weeks, until he was granted the status of political refugee by the German embassy in Belgrade. They gave him a *Fremdenpass*, which allowed him to travel to Germany and work there.

'The two of us were supposed to leave together, but earlier that year, two people had been killed while trying to cross the Danube. Their bodies were given back to their families, who lived in the little village of Sibiu. Grigore was shocked and terrified, and decided to postpone his escape. His desire to find what he called "*Mein Weg in die Freiheit*" was too strong, though.'

'*His path in freedom*. That's a beautiful expression. What happened to him?'

'Grigore's been working for a company that makes orthopedic mattresses ever since he arrived in Germany. He lives in the city of Rosenheim, in Bavaria. All this time he's put money aside until he could finally build a house for his parents back in Romania, at the foot of the Carpathian mountains.'

'What a wonderful story!'

'Yes,' Mr Kiss says, sighing. 'I guess Grigore, you, and I were pretty lucky. I think I was, at least. And not only because I managed to flee Romania. Not that I regret growing up there, by the way. I love my country, and I know how much it gave me.'

'That's true, we're pretty lucky. But you said you moved around a lot?'

'Yes, my journey didn't end in Paris. As soon as I got my papers, I said goodbye to my adoptive French family and took off. First I went to Montreal. The cold was unbearable, but Canada was like an El Dorado for me, a land of opportunity, and a true melting pot of cultures. I met people from all over the world there, who immediately made me feel like I belonged. And I met Japanese artists, too. One of them was a tattoo master who'd studied at a famous school in Tokyo. He gave classes in his workshop for next to nothing, and I never missed one, learning all I could about the art of tattooing. He saw my potential, what had led to my being something of a 'frustrated artist' back in Romania.'

'What did you do next?'

'I moved to Tokyo to become a professional tattooist. It was the best decision I ever made, after leaving Romania. My experience in Tokyo was enriching, even though it wasn't always easy at first. After my time in Canada, the Japanese seemed quite xenophobic. It took months for me to be allowed to sign a lease for a tiny apartment, just a small room. People tend to be prejudiced against tattoo artists, and of course I was also a foreigner. In Japan, some people even think only gang members get tattoos. Do you like tattoos?' he suddenly asks, turning towards me.

I don't really know what to answer.

I see how much he loves life, and what fond memories he still has of his early life behind the Iron Curtain. He may have had to overcome a lot of obstacles, but he isn't at all bitter. He just wants to continue his journey without having to let go of the past. As for me, I've made the deliberate choice never to dwell on my past, to pretend it didn't exist even. Yet there's a void inside me. I know that's not the way Mr Kiss feels. He never deviated from the path he chose for himself, whereas I've devoted so much of my energy towards reshaping myself into a new person in a new environment. Maybe it was just an instinctive act of self-preservation, but as we speak, I realise that something is missing in my life, something as important as the air I breathe. I've buried the past, yet doing so only made the foundation of my future unstable. What we are is intrinsically linked to the place we were born; our sense of identity is such that even if we leave our birthplace behind, never to return, there always remains something deep inside of us that draws us irresistibly to our roots. And I can tell that Mr Kiss, even though he's travelled the world and experienced all sorts of things, has never turned his back on his roots.

Our roots they grow, invisible and free,
Anchored in the subterranean depths,
Watching, unmoving, as we waver above,
Silent powers that elude our gaze
While we follow our own paths, freed of everything.

They're generous, our roots,
Waiting, ready to relieve us,
Watching over us with benevolence,
Aware of the truth that hides in their core.

They watch us, passive but always patient,
They remain always sincere,
For they know that time is in their favour.

For they know, our roots,
They wait and guide us, unaware, towards them,
Mindless, instinctive forces
Whose attraction we can't resist.

For they know, our roots,
That there always comes a day
When our lives lead us back to them,
Our threads intertwined yet again.
Then, safe in their warm embrace,
We feel happiness wash over us
And wash away pain and regrets
As our own interior paradise is finally revealed.

7:10 pm

I can't stop thinking about Mr Kiss's question about tattoos. I guess there's something about them that intrigues me, and I can imagine how exhilarating it must feel to get tattooed. More so today than when I was a student in Berlin. Getting a tattoo is like partaking in a ritual, which is what I find so attractive about it. Then there's this sort of secretive side to it still, this almost taboo aspect, which only makes it more alluring. As an art form, it seems to have limitless potential.

Tattoos are like a secret language. Getting a tattoo isn't the kind of decision you make lightly, thought has to go into it. You better come up with something you know you won't ever tire of or, worse, be ashamed of a few years down the road.

It's not a minor gesture. The only thing I found exciting about tattoos back then was their erotic dimension, which I've always found fascinating. It's an intimate act, you're letting a stranger draw something on your body.

A needle against the skin, a powerful alliance of energy and desire. Like crossing the border into the unknown just for the sake of it. Tattoo artists are open-minded individuals, willing to explore new areas of the body and mind, forbidden by society.

I can relate to Mr Kiss's fascination with his tattoo master, and the friendship that can develop between a mentor and an eager student.

'Yes,' I finally say, 'I guess I do like tattoos. Do tattooing methods differ between cultures?'

'Yes, there are differences. In some cultures, tattoos are still created by hand-tapping the ink into the skin. Many artists nowadays use tattoo machines, though. The first one was invented towards the end of the nineteenth century, if I remember correctly; today they use electro-magnetic coils. I prefer to work with my hands and bamboo or steel needles rather than with machines. It's a traditional Japanese method they call *horimono*. Did you know that we've found evidence that tattoos have existed since the Neolithic Era?'

'Really? That's unbelievable.'

I can't imagine Martín's reaction if I came home one day with a tattoo. Martín's a true scientist, he doesn't care for the visual arts all that much. I'm sure seeing me with a tattoo would be quite the cultural shock for him.

Back before the Wall fell, there were a lot of South American students and social workers in East Berlin. The city had a cosmopolitan student community, and foreigners got along perfectly well with the natives, or *Ossies*, as the West Germans called us. It was a cultural metropolis, which in turn prompted even more people from all over the world to go study and work there. That's actually how I met Martín: he studied microbiology at Humboldt University and did odd jobs as a social worker, whilst I was getting a masters in History and a degree in Spanish. That was a few years after my devastating breakup, the complete collapse of my relationship with my tenor. I couldn't have found someone more different if I'd tried. I guess I was attracted to him as a reaction to my previous relationship, but it was also a way of shedding my previous identity as a would-be rebel. I needed an important change in my life. Getting a tattoo wouldn't have been a problem if I'd still been with my tenor, but with Martín, it was out of the question!

7:11 pm

We just passed the old brick building of the Lycée Carnot on the Boulevard Malesherbes. Just across from it is the National School of Music of Paris, which always reminds me of East German architecture, a symbol of my country's glorious past. There's a clear difference in Berlin between those buildings built before the partition of Germany, and those built after. Berlin had ceased to be the country's capital after the signing of the Warsaw Pact, a few years before I was born. Had it been up to me, I would never have chosen to be born in Germany, or in Paris for that matter. It's not as if French History didn't have its fair share of dark moments, especially back then. I'm thinking for instance of the massacre of October 17, 1961, when the police launched a violent assault against a peaceful pro-FLN demonstration. Things have changed since then, and nowadays demonstrations are an almost everyday occurrence. The traffic on the Left Bank of the Seine, by the Palais Bourbon, is often a nightmare due to some demonstration or other.

Every morning I go talk to Monsieur Pierre, who runs the newsstand across the street from our apartment. We've known each other for over twenty years, and have become friends. He's pushing sixty and always in black. He wears his brown hair long, and a small pair of glasses make him look something of an intellectual. He's an avid reader who knows everything about what's on display on his shelves. He's also a sculptor, and never loses his fantastic sense of humour.

One day I was standing with him chatting away, like usual. He was proudly showing me pictures of a sculpture he had made with materials he'd found washed ashore. It looked like a conceptual *chaise longue*!

An old lady approached and stood behind us without saying a word. I felt uncomfortable and turned towards her and in a friendly voice I said:

'Hello, how are you?'

She responded succinctly:

'I think therefore I am'

That was quite a statement for a casual encounter at our local's newsstand! We then started a conversation based on her comment and entered a philosophical world. She described herself as a disciple and student of Lacan and how she had practised psychoanalysis for years. She looked frail but her personality was overwhelming and strong. She made her point clear that Lacan's variation of Descartes 'I think therefore I am' made more sense. It was the first time I'd heard that but I ended up agreeing with her.

I've always enjoyed those moments of intimacy with strangers. Chance encounters are what makes Paris such a unique place for people like Mr Kiss and me.

The main difference between East Germany and France is precisely this wealth of ideas. Each of us is free to question anything we don't agree with, from politics to school curriculums. In fact, it's our civic duty. It's so refreshing not to have to weigh each and every word, to be able to freely say what we mean. All authoritarian regimes, of course, begin by abolishing that freedom, in order to control opposition movements and to consolidate their own power.

7:12 pm

'Do you know who these statues are supposed to be?' I ask Mr Kiss as we cross the Place du Général-Catroux, which looks like a square without being one.

'People call it the Place des Trois Dumas, because of the three statues that represent members of Alexandre Dumas's family.'

'You really do know everything about Paris!'

I reach into my purse for my blush compact and inspect myself in the mirror. I really need to freshen up a little. I look a little tired, and I have bags under my eyes. I put blush on my cheeks and anti-wrinkle cream on my face. The sun hasn't been kind to my hair colouring. I have to go down to the hairdresser – my music adviser, as I call him. I love to go have my hair dyed, not only because I like seeing him, but also because I enjoy spending hours just talking about music with him. He is an expert on pop music, including all sorts of anecdotes about even the most obscure artists.

I wish my hair looked better for my son's birthday party. My roots are growing out, but I'm afraid there isn't much I can do about it right now. I'll only have time to take a quick shower and dress for the party when I get home; I guess I'll just have to put my hair up tonight.

I wonder if my tenor would recognise me if we were to run into each other in the street; after all, I've changed a lot since the last time he saw me. It's weird how this conversation with Mr Kiss is bringing me back to East Berlin and to my life with him. Our story comes bubbling back to the surface, it makes me want to search for him, for any sign of life. To know the warmth of his embrace again, after all these years. Of course, there remains this insurmountable gap between the past and the present. Whenever one feels ready to plumb the depths of one's own heart, though, is always the right time to do it. Feelings don't obey any kind of temporal law. They float freely and reappear at will, as long as they're strong enough to survive the passage of time and the weight of memory.

We just drove past the entrance to the Parc Monceau, with its gilded gates. It's a majestic place, but one that, somehow, also feels very intimate.

Am I running late? I better call home to make sure everything's going well. I hope the cook will have had time to finish everything, and that the stores will still be open when I get there. Perhaps I should ask Elinor to go buy the few things I need instead. I got so carried away by our conversation that I forgot all about the time.

It's not an unpleasant feeling, though, to lose track of time that way. I feel better, as if I were just waking up from a good nap. It's weird, how that works, how we can feel more alert after losing sense of everything for a while.

Now we're stuck in traffic on the Boulevard Malesherbes. The car's not even moving. Perhaps we could stop on the way somewhere so that I can buy the last few things for tonight.

'Would you mind stopping at a grocery store for a few minutes? There are a couple things I need to pick up before going home.'

'I'll try to remember. We can stop Rue du Bac, right before Boulevard Raspail. We could be another half hour, though, with the traffic.'

'Sure.'

He looks at his watch, an old-fashioned gold-and-steel model. Clearly he's trying to figure out a way for me not to be late. He's such a thoughtful person!

'They say time is precious, but I don't believe it for a minute,' Mr Kiss says.

'Why not?'

'Well, I don't think it does heal all wounds.'

'Maybe not, but it numbs you, and sometimes that's enough to forget.'

Then again, when I think of the impact time has had on my own modest life, I am forced to recognise it barely had any effect at all.

'Time can be deceiving, too. Waiting for it to solve all your problems is just another way not to make decisions.'

'I guess you're right. I'd never thought about it that way. But don't you think sometimes one has to take one's time, when faced with important decisions?'

El tiempo te engaña, time makes a fool out of you. Those words echo in my head, although I can't remember who said them.

'But sometimes taking one's time means waiting until an even less convenient moment to solve one's problems,' he says. 'Sometimes it means letting one's problems accumulate instead of trying to solve them at once. And sometimes, time feels like it will never pass.'

I cannot but agree with Mr Kiss's arguments. I'm both surprised and delighted to find us now talking about this. What matters, I think, isn't so much time, as the moment. The perfect moment.

Time can be so fleeting, yet so rich. It flows only one way, but who hasn't ever wished it could flow backwards? Time doesn't care about us. It gives and takes, but it often takes way more than it gives back. We spend so much energy just trying to resist it. But as time passes, what remains of even a kiss?

Perhaps Mr Kiss knows. I don't want the thread that ties us to each other to break, so I return to our conversation. 'Would you mind telling me more about your life in Japan?'

'Of course not. Once I was settled in Tokyo, I continued studying with another tattoo master. I began to let my own creativity come out, to open myself up to new opportunities. For a while, I focused on the trees and flowers of Japan. I have a passion for nature, and I thought that, if I wanted to learn as much as I could about Japanese culture, I should study their natural environment and the way they interact with it and are inspired by it. I've always been fascinated by bonsai trees, and I wanted to understand why the Japanese care so much about them. I hoped thus to be able to touch and feel the soul of this country I'd decided to make mine for a while.

'Nature is a key aspect of Japanese culture. You'll find it in their paintings, in their poetry, even in Japanese calligraphy. They're introverted people – it's the way most of them were raised – and I thought that would be a more subtle way to understand their way of life. So I starting reading all I could find about the plants, trees, and flowers of the Japanese islands.

'One day a young Japanese woman, of maybe twenty-five years old, came in and stood by the little reception desk. She was very prim and proper. She didn't seem entirely at ease, as if she wasn't quite sure what she was doing there. My master nodded at me, his way of saying I should go see what she wanted.

'I was right, she wasn't entirely sure about getting a tattoo. Not wanting to intimidate her further or scare her away by showing her the workshop right away, I asked her to come to the studio with me. After a while the conversation shifted to plants and flowers. I read her a few haikus, told her to meditate on nature's beauty and the way it manifests itself. I told her she should take her time, and only return once she was certain. I promised her I'd be there to take care of her when she did come back. She didn't say much, but her eyes spoke for her.'

7:17 pm
We're now on the Place Saint-Augustin, seat of one of the most beautiful churches in Paris. I always take the time to look at it when I'm in the area. Its architecture is unique: if you look at its ceiling when inside, you can see the building's metallic structure.

'I love this church,' I say. 'It's gorgeous.'

'Yes. Did you know it was built on the ruins of an old chapel from the fourth century?'

Mr Kiss has got to be the most erudite taxi driver I've ever met!

'Anyway, she came back about a week later,' he says, answering my question even before I can articulate it. 'From the moment she came through the door, I knew I was in love with her. It's strange to see one's feelings change from a sort of protective instinct to a much deeper desire. She was shrouded in mystery. She told me she wanted me to tattoo a cherry blossom on her shoulder blade. When I did, it was like an oath we were both taking, an oath of love that would unite us forever. An admission of our deep desire to belong to each other. I'd never experienced such a sudden attraction, one that seemed to come from some faraway place within me. Perhaps it was this protective instinct that drove me to her; I felt this vulnerability in her, and I was unable to resist. I still love her the same way I did on that first day.'

Mr Kiss remains silent for a brief moment, then goes on with his story. 'The cherry blossom is part of Japanese culture. It symbolises the fleeting beauty of life. It's even used as an emblem by the military. The kamikazes used to paint cherry blossoms on their planes before flying off on their missions, too. The Japanese believed that the souls of their dead soldiers would be reincarnated as cherry blossoms. There are more than a few poems on the subject, actually.'

7:18 pm

Even though the window's still open, it's getting hotter and hotter inside the cab as we draw closer to the centre of Paris. I stick my head out the window, hoping for a cool breeze on my face. I struggle to get out of my khaki summer jacket, under which I'm wearing a green t-shirt. I then fold my jacket carefully; I'm a little OCD when it comes to my clothes. My husband and children never fail to tease me about it, either. When it comes to packing suitcases, though, no one can beat me. I fold everything perfectly and use tissue paper to protect the most delicate items. This way I manage to fit in twice as much as most people.

The silence has gotten a little awkward, but a moment of silence in the middle of a conversation can be enlightening. I'm still glad the radio's not on. I hate commercials and traffic updates, and the news that get repeated over and over again. Some drivers like to talk radio programmes, which is even worse.

I don't mind outside noises, though. Each place has its own sonic atmosphere, so to speak. Geneva, Paris, and New Delhi, for instance, sound nothing like one another. You could make a game out of that, trying to recognise different places only by ear. If you're used to the sounds of a particular place, it can't be that difficult.

Training one's ear to identify the differences between the two types of ambient noises, soft ones and hard, aggressive ones, would be quite a challenge. Perhaps that would allow us to hear things in the silence, though, things we're usually unable to perceive. I'm thinking of John Cage's *4'33"*, during which the conductor and the orchestra remain completely silent through the piece's three movements. The point is for the audience to listen to all ambient sounds and integrate them to the piece.

Sounds are an integral part of our day. If I close my eyes, I can let them guide me. I am thrilled to let them carry me away and stimulate my imagination. Sounds are like smells, they can bring back specific moments with great clarity. Much more so than images, which are more easily lost in the countless visual stimuli we receive every day.

Another police siren goes off, interrupting this fleeting instant of serenity. I jump again, I must be more trau-matised than I thought.

'There must have been some kind of accident,' Mr Kiss says. 'I doubt this traffic's due to a demonstration. It's the middle of August, after all. Everyone's on holiday.'

7:20 pm

'Have you ever heard of the Japanese belief that a person's blood type has a considerable influence on his or her personality?' asks Mr Kiss.

'I don't think so, I would remember it.'

'I was surprised when I heard about it, too.'

'Tell me more.'

'According to that theory, there exists in the blood some sort of markers that correspond to different personality types. Worse, though, they also let it figure out whether two people are compatible or not. It was an American pathologist of Austrian descent who discovered blood types at the beginning of the twentieth century. Karl Landsteiner, his name was. It was a revolution in the field of medicine, changing forever the way blood transfusions were performed. Before that, many people used to die from being transfused with blood that wasn't compatible with theirs.'

The name Landsteiner does ring a bell. I refrain from commenting, though, sensing that Mr Kiss has more to say about this strange theory.

'Does that mean your blood type is determined by your ethnicity?' I ask.

'Some studies show that's partly the case, yeah. Asians, for instance, are more likely to have type B blood.'

'What about the Japanese theory?'

'In 1927, a Japanese professor named Furukawa conducted a study that would prove very popular and become a reference in spite of its total lack of scientific basis. Some conservative families still believe in it as a way of determining a person's character by looking at his or her blood type, and whether a man and a woman are compatible life partners.'

I'm not quite sure I know where he's going with this. I'll have to ask Martín about it, he must have heard of it.

'Many Japanese stars list their blood type in their biographies, along with their astrological sign or the colour of their eyes,' Mr Kiss says. 'Video game creators often do the same for their games' characters! These ideas entered popular culture back in the '70s, and they've taken an almost insane importance.'

'This is amazing, I had no idea!'

'Our blood types aren't compatible.'

It takes me a moment to understand he's talking about the young Japanese woman he met at the tattoo parlour.

'Her name's Sachi, but I still call her "Cherry Blossom". She used to ask me questions about anything and everything. She shared my outlook on life, trusted me completely. That's still the case, I think. She'd never met anyone from Romania before, and was very curious about my culture. She had started to learn Romanian, so I gave her Eugène Ionesco's *The Bald Soprano*, the play inspired by the absurdities of foreign language teaching methods.'

'It must seem even weirder to the Japanese, I suppose. After all, their language is based on an entirely different system.'

'In any case, you don't learn about a culture simply by learning the language. It's all very artificial. Language is nothing but a tool.'

'What I like most about *The Bald Soprano* is the way it becomes more and more absurd as it goes along. There's even a laugh track at some point, except it's only used when what's going on isn't funny at all.'

'That was very hard for Sachi to understand, actually. The Japanese aren't used to laughing at things that aren't supposed to be funny.'

'You two seem to have shared a lot of your cultural experiences.'

'That's the way it was right from the start. It's what makes our relationship work, really. The first book she gave me was Kazuo Ishiguro's *Never Let Me Go*. She told me she hadn't read it, but she found the title appropriate.'

'That's quite a love message.'

I'm touched by the way Mr Kiss is opening up about his relationship with Sachi, but I can't help but be a little upset as well, as it reminds me of my own unfinished story.

I wonder if I'm not still looking for my tenor, even subconsciously. Sometimes when I least expect it, images from the past come rushing back, and I realise he never really left my life.

'I'm taking you somewhere, and I won't take no for an answer,' he said one day. 'It's an hour's drive from Berlin.'

'Wait, when are we leaving?'

'Tomorrow afternoon. We'll be back the next day.'

My heart was already racing.

'I read about that place in a guidebook, I thought you'd like it.'

We left at about four thirty the next day, then an hour and a half later we were in a village by the name of Bestensee. We parked in the main square, then went looking for our hotel.

The light was soft, the late afternoon sky all pale pink and fuchsia. We eventually found our inn after asking someone on our way. Every single one of the place's eight bedrooms had a view of the lake. The inn was surrounded by trees, it felt like a dream. We spent the evening walking under the starry sky, and when we got back, we found that someone had placed lit candles everywhere in our room. I wish I could have stayed there with him forever.

He's still with me wherever I go. Even after all these years, I find myself asking him questions, as if I subconsciously wanted to know what he thinks about what's going on in my life. His voice sounds like it's coming from far away, from somewhere deep inside me, supporting me in everything I do. He's an invisible presence that's never left me.

7:26 pm

I need to take my mind off him. I take the *Herald Tribune* out of my bag and go looking for the article I was reading on the plane. 'The Puzzle of Rossini's Brief Career'.

I like reading the headlines, it always reminds me of that Pakistani news dealer who works in Saint-Germain-des-Prés, going from café to café to tell people the news they actually want to hear. He just makes everything up. I can hear his voice in my head, shouting the imaginary headlines he knows will shock and delight people. He should be awarded an honorary psychology degree. He's so adept at manipulating words, so clever about it, that even though everyone knows his stories are made up, you can't help but believe them for half a second. I don't know who could have done that kind of thing in East Germany.

That *Herald Tribune* article is about Rossini, of course,

but more generally about the incomprehensible phenomena that sometimes happens inside us. How else do you explain that one of the greatest composers of all times suddenly decided to put an end to his career, turning his back on fame and glory to spend the rest of his life in seclusion and silence? *William Tell*, his thirty-ninth opera, had just been a smashing success when Rossini decided to stop composing in 1829. He was only thirty-seven years old. There's nothing else like it in the history of music. According to the article, Stendhal once wrote that everyone was talking about Rossini's farewell to music, 'from Moscow to Naples, from London to Vienna, from Paris to Calcutta.'

It's an upsetting article that evokes Rossini's deep suffering, the incomprehension and frustration he must have felt. He left Paris ten days after the premiere of *William Tell*, never to return. Why do we sometimes find ourselves plunged into such despair?

Mr Kiss's situation must be no less frustrating. Apparently we as human beings can now be categorised according to our blood type. Why do we always feel that urge to come up with a rational explanation for those phenomena we cannot understand? I'm one to talk, of course, with my inability to let go of the past.

7:35 pm

'Take a look at her picture,' Mr Kiss says.

He hands me his phone, with a picture of a young woman on the screen. Her skin is smooth and delicate,

53

and I can't tell how old she is. That's often the case with Asians; whatever wrinkles they get are barely visible, and they look much younger than they actually are. As if time had no grasp on them whatsoever.

Her face is like an angel's, her smile painfully sweet. Her hair is up in a messy bun. She's wearing a deep blue shirt, cut to fit well at the waist. It's a little wrinkled, but that looks like a deliberate choice rather than neglect. It gives her a unique, trendy look. She's obviously a nonconformist, but at the same time she doesn't dare completely break away from tradition, perhaps because she doesn't want to reveal just how sharp she is. It feels odd to be able, or think yourself able, to pick up so much about someone from a single photograph. Especially someone you've never actually met. Not as odd as thinking you can guess someone's personality traits simply by looking at his or her blood type, though.

A portrait such as that one is always a product of the moment it was taken. There's a history behind it, and that history seems to show through the picture, granting the person in it a sort of revealing aura. Within every image there is a hidden world, full of intimate messages that it's possible to pick up on if one takes the necessary time to dig a little deeper into what's actually there. So it goes with text as well; a simple passage can reveal things about how its author felt when he wrote it. Those moments we end up being, almost accidentally privy contain countless secrets.

'She's very pretty. She seems sweet.'

It's a pretty short commentary, considering everything I think I just figured out about her, but I don't think Mr Kiss expects a detailed psychological analysis.

What does he expect me to say, though?

Showing me her photograph was a way to nudge the conversation.

I oblige, then: 'Is she in Paris right now?'

'Unfortunately, no. She's still in Tokyo, working for her father. He's a carpenter, a master of seals. It's an ancient Japanese tradition. She's learning the art of Kiwari, a construction code from the seventeenth century based on the golden ratio. There are many different Kiwari systems, all passed from one generation to the next.'

'From what I've heard, wood is the main construction material used in Japan, right?'

'Yes. They use mostly pine, cedar, and cypress. But they also import wood from other countries, they call it "precious foreign wood". See, even wood bears a different title when it's foreign. At least it's considered precious, though, unlike foreign men. I'm afraid I speak from experience.'

I look out the window. My attention is drawn to the majestic chestnut trees that line the Boulevard Malesherbes on both sides. The traffic is still dense, but I can hear birds singing.

I let my mind take me to one of those wooden Japanese

structures where everything is serene and quiet. Such purity and inspiration! And such a fragile equilibrium. Adding even one new element can shatter the purity of a place and disturb its harmony. A noisy heating unit, for instance, would obviously be out of the question. Stillness and calm are only achievable in the absence of all those machines we rely on for comfort. Artificial noises are the bane of this architecture philosophy, and should be banned outright.

7:38 pm

I mustn't forget the candles. There should be candles everywhere in the apartment tonight; it's a party after all! I better buy some glasses now, too. I'm not sure I'll have time to stop by the neighbours' to borrow some, what with all this traffic. Plus, it would be impolite to drop by without staying a bit to talk with them, and I'm sure they would be curious to know all about my trip to Greece. There's a grocery store on the way, though, closer than the one on Rue du Bac, if I'm not mistaken. Perhaps I should just go there now.

'Can we please stop for ten minutes, I really need to do some shopping before I get home.'

'Of course. I'll stop by the next store.'

Thinking about my son's birthday now, I feel like a cold sweat's trickling down my back. A few years ago, fate spared Lukas by a mere few minutes. We were spending the summer in London, staying at one of my cousins'. Lukas was coming home from a friend's on a

Saturday morning, but when he got to the tube station, he realised the entrance was blocked. There were sirens going off all over the city, no one knew precisely what was happening, everyone was beginning to panic. It was the morning of July 7, 2005.

People were trying to call their friends and families on their mobile phones, but the network was overloaded and no one could get through. I'd heard the news of the attack, and a searing intuition jerked me out of my morning torpor. Panic crippled me, leaving me unable to do anything, unable to even think. Martín was away on a research trip, I was on my own, and I didn't know what to do. I must have called Lukas's phone at least fifty times in a row. My hands were shaking so much I kept hitting the wrong keys. He never picked up. Something told me he must have been in the middle of the bombings, but I didn't know which Tube line he was supposed to take, and I didn't have his friend's number. I had no idea when he would have left there, and no way to find out. Why did he have to wake up so early when we were on vacation? The question made no sense, of course, but in my panic I couldn't stop thinking about it. As if it was the cause of the despair I felt taking over me.

I wasn't alone in my distress, of course. In a matter of seconds, an attack not unlike 9/11 had shaken the entire British capital.

The hours that followed were excruciating, a mother's nightmare. Then, at about 11:30, the doorbell rang, and I rushed to it. Lukas was standing there, safe and sound.

He had no idea about what had happened. He'd just noticed that the entire centre of London was blocked off, and had had to walk for two and a half hours before finally finding a bus to take him back. A guardian angel must have been looking over him that day.

7:39 pm

'See there? Number 9, Boulevard Malesherbes?' I say, in an attempt to show Mr Kiss that I, too, know my share of anecdotes about Paris. 'Marcel Proust and his family used to live there, from 1873 to 1900. Can you believe that Proust used to walk these streets right here, across from that advertising column? Back then there was a Cerisier bakery there, too.'

'Cerisier, really? That's funny!'

'You've heard of that, too?' I said, astonished.

'No, not at all. The name just reminds me of Sachi's tattoo, that's all.'

'Yes, of course. Sorry, I didn't think. I hope you don't mind my coming back to it, but this whole thing about judging people by their blood type has been bothering me ever since you mentioned it. As it happens, my husband works for the Institut Pasteur as a scientist. You said the original study was made by a Japanese scientist, right?'

'Yes, Takeji Furukawa. It's fascinating stuff, really, but it's got no basis in science whatsoever.'

'But you said people in Japan really do believe it?'

'Yes. There are even some in the Ministry of Foreign

Affairs who believe that only type O blood individuals make good diplomats.'

'You can't be serious!'

'Unfortunately, I am. For many, it's become a dangerous obsession. Some people wouldn't think of recruiting new employees or marrying someone without first looking at their blood types. Believe me, I know what I'm talking about. Some kindergartens even put children into different groups based on their blood types. And of course, many dating agencies use it as a criteria when matching people.'

'Is it as big as something like astrology, then?'

'Actually, I think that to many Japanese, it is more reliable than astrology. They treat it as if it were actual science. And once a specific blood type has been condemned, for whatever reason, there's little you can do about it.'

I often saw my tenor after class. We would listen to music together, and talk about our project of opening a free, or almost free, opera house, so that absolutely everyone could come. We'd been lucky enough to be able to hear the best operas for next to nothing in East Germany, and we knew how educational it was to do so from an early age. That project was a dream we shared. One of many, actually. We had so many, back then. We'd meet at my Marienburger Strasse palace, as I liked to call it, which I'd furnished with the help of my friends. We'd sit around the fireplace and warm our bodies and souls. I felt incredibly strong then, as if everything were possible. He protected me while at the same time making me feel free and independent. He opened my eyes to a world where love reigned supreme and where we could build a future together.

From the moment I met him, I felt the urge to impress him, so that he would find me inspiring. There was nothing I could teach him about music, of course, so I had to find something else. I wanted him to see me as an adult, but I was still a child. I would talk to him about the world I lived in, the world of young girls my age, and I like to think he was genuinely interested. He was like a sponge, absorbing everything I told him. One day he showed up with a present, a pair of red and white high-heeled shoes he'd had a friend buy in the West. You couldn't find such wonders anywhere in the East. I was blown away. He paid attention to everything and often knew what I wanted before I even did. Another day he came home with a chocolate bar – or half of it, since he'd eaten the other half on the way. It was my favourite brand, one that was hard to find and that I'd mentioned only once before. He'd remembered it, though. In return, the only way I could think of to show him how much I admired him was to learn as much as I could about the things that fascinated him. As my love for him grew, I studied ever harder.

I wonder what I would have done if I'd been told that our blood types weren't compatible, if all my dreams and ambitions had been taken away from me overnight in such a manner.

I don't want to let myself drown in memories and nostalgia. I need Mr Kiss to throw me a life belt.

'Romania has a strong artistic tradition, doesn't it?'

'It sure does. But it was almost impossible to earn a living as an artist there. Under Ceausescu's regime, the arts weren't exactly considered a priority. Every industry in the country had been nationalised, to comply with the wishes of the USSR. Same with our natural resources. Corruption was rampant, and it's the Romanian people who paid the price of the government's austerity programme. About two million people were persecuted or killed under the communist regime between 1945 and 1989, so I'll let you imagine how violently artistic expression may have been repressed back then.

'That was no country for artists, really. And to think that before the communists came to power, the Bucharest National University of Arts was known throughout the world. People like Brancusi learned their craft there, although of course, it was in Paris that Brancusi started working as a sculptor, in Rodin's workshop. That was in 1904, wasn't it? Anyway, two months later, he was leaving. He'd already developed his own style and language.

'Believe it or not, there are actually strong artistic connections between Paris, Bucharest, and Tokyo. The great Japanese-American sculptor Isamu Noguchi once worked as an assistant in Brancusi's workshop in Paris, where he learned how to sculpt stone and wood. I told you that Sachi's father is a carpenter and a mason, right?

Well, I thought about giving him a book on Brancusi as a present, to help forge our own connection like the ones that exist between Romanian, French, and Japanese artists. It was no use, though. It was like talking to a wall, really.'

An image of Brancusi's *Maiastra* suddenly pops into my head. It's a golden bird which, according to the legend, can predict the future. I wish I knew mine.

'Do you know Brancusi's *Maiastra*?' Mr Kiss asks.

I look at him suspiciously in the rear-view mirror. Does this man have telepathic powers?

'You read my mind, I was just thinking about it.'

'How strange indeed. Anyway, I've always been intrigued by the stories about that golden bird. I often wonder just how much control we have over our own future, and what credence we should give to omens and predictions.'

He remains silent for a while then, as if pondering something. 'My future with Sachi is more than uncertain,' he finally says. 'We have no choice but to trust in Providence. Do you think it's possible to change one's blood type?'

It's a strange question, but Mr Kiss's grave expression confirms it is a serious one.

'You really should ask my husband. I've mentioned that he works at the Institut Pasteur, right? I could ask him to look into it for you, if you want.'

I was already feeling a connection with Mr Kiss because

we're both wandering souls, exiles from the East come to Paris to start a new life, but now I see we have something else in common, as we both carry the burden of an impossible love. The difference, of course, is that he refuses to accept his situation as hopeless, when I buried my love long ago, without even giving it a chance.

7:45 pm

All I've got left is a souvenir box. I managed to stuff my entire past into one, the same way I manage to stuff everything I need into suitcases. I'm good at it, I've had practice. It's as if I'd known that one day, all those memories would be the only thing from my past I'd be able to keep with me. Or would want to keep with me, perhaps. It was like an intuition, or perhaps just an urge to keep things that had no value whatsoever to anyone but me. Drawings by some of my school friends, for instance, or tickets to places I'd been.

Memories of him as well, of course. The red and white shoes, some letters, a few pictures of the two of us together. Recordings of his voice he'd given me, programmes and tickets to operas we'd seen together, small wooden figurines we'd bought at the Christmas market one year. I remember one in particular, a wooden Santa Claus flying above the clouds, one leg all the way up against his chest and the other trailing behind him, a sack filled to the brim with presents on his back. He'd bought it for me one cold December evening, as we were walking down the Oranien Strasse in search of a place to have a glass of mulled wine and something to eat. We stopped in front of a toy store on the way. Every item in the window was made of wood, and when we went in, I felt like Alice entering Wonderland. It was magical. There was a sort of small branch by the cash register, the sort they usually put little angels on, except on top of that one there was no angel, but Santa Claus. He grabbed it and told me he wanted to buy it for me. All those years I've kept it carefully hidden in that box, but now I'd like to take it out, and give it its old life back.

On November 9, 1989, at 10:30 at night, Checkpoint Charlie on the Friedrichstrasse was opened. A moment that would last forever. As the Berlin Wall was falling, I had to make a crucial decision: now that the doors to the free world were opening for me, should I go and explore it? Back then I didn't have the courage. I guess that's why I've never opened my little souvenir box again.

7:48 pm

'There's a grocery store right there. If you want to do some shopping, I can stop here.'

Mr Kiss's deep voice seems to be coming from far away. I'm still lost somewhere in East Germany, I've forgotten all about the Parisian traffic. I'm glad he hasn't, though.

'Thank you, Monsieur Kiss. I shouldn't be longer than ten minutes.'

He smiles at me. I grab my purse and empty it of all magazines and books, which I leave on the back seat. I allow myself one cigarette before going in. I started smoking the day he left me, and I've never been able to stop.

In the end, our relationship lasted less than a year. A few during which we withdrew from reality. He came to see me as often as his work would allow, and when he did, our lives became a whirlwind. I lost all sense of time when I was in his arms. *La dolce vita*, he called it, our life away from life.

He would always wait for me in a different spot after class. We'd get in his small car, and the moment I climbed into it, I would forget everything else. My whole world would dissolve into those few hours during which I abandoned myself to his love. Just hearing his voice gave me thrills that resonated deep into my soul.

I toss the cigarette butt away to enter the store, but I realise I've forgotten what it is I want to buy, and I've left the list I made in the cab. I suddenly find myself unable to focus. Lost, I turn around and make my way back to the taxi. Mr Kiss is clearly surprised to see me back so soon, and empty-handed.

'Are you all right?' he asks.

I really don't know what to say.

7:53 pm

He turned the radio on while I was outside, and Aretha Franklin's 'You Make Me Feel Like a Natural Woman' is playing. 'My soul was in the lost and found,' she sings, and that's exactly how I felt after my tenor left me.

I try to collect my thoughts.

'Thank you, but it was just too crowded. I guess I'll have to do my shopping later. I think I'd prefer to go straight home, OK?'

Perhaps Mr Kiss knows what I'm going through. He knows that pain always comes back when we least expect it.

I settle back into the taxi and pick up the issue of *Le Monde des livres* I'd discarded earlier. I hadn't noticed the title of the article I was reading: 'I love you more than words can say', a reference to an Otis Redding song.

The article is about Karen Dalton, a legendary singer associated with many great artists like Bob Dylan. She did a cover of the Otis Redding song, changing the meaning of the words so that it would fit her own story. All of a sudden I want to share that article with Mr Kiss.

'There's an article in there I think you'll like,' I say. 'It's about the way some songs can affect us deeply, how they speak of our pain and of our inability to heal.'

'Really? That does sound interesting. Thank you.'

There were all those letters I never sent him, too. I didn't have his address, I didn't know where he was, not even if he was still in Europe or on another continent altogether. What's the point of writing letters if you can't ever send them?

I've never read them again, but I still remember exactly what I wrote. I didn't ask him any question, even though there were so many I would have wished him to answer:

Why did you leave me?

Why didn't you say anything?

What did you expect me to do, since you gave me no choice in the matter?

Will I ever love anyone the way I loved you?

When did you decide you were going to leave me?

Did you tell anyone else about it?

Do you think you acted fairly towards me?

Did you ever wonder how I felt?

Do you think deciding to have an abortion was an easy thing for me to?

How could you say you loved me and hurt me so much?

What was it that was more important to you than our love?

I haven't been able to listen to the music we used to listen to together. What about you?

How will you remember me? And how do you think I'll remember you?

What I've kept from all this is thousands of memories and every second of our time together. I keep you within me, you're a part of me I could never get rid of. You're like an invisible friend, always there with me.

Those questions became irrelevant as soon as you made your choice, though. A decision as final as yours leaves no place for interrogations. So instead of questions, I began my first letter with a quote by W. B. Yeats, 'before the world was made,' and ended it with another one by Balzac, 'Women are ever the dupes or victims of their extreme sensitiveness.' Because in times of great distress, our own words are sometimes not enough.

I'm even more upset than I'd realised. I'd buried all those painful memories deep within me, and up until now I'd always refused to unearth them and face the consequences. Life taught me that you should always look ahead, that you should always hope for the best while accepting that you can't change your own fate. The Berlin Wall fell, I married a man I fell in love with, and he gave me two children I cherish more than my own life. But although I'd managed to bury the passion that had once consumed me, it had never truly gone away. Worse still, it had kept growing silently, without my being aware of it. Yet I think I've always known that one day, something would bring it back, would allow it to reappear stronger than ever. Today's the day. Here and now, in this cab. It's such an upsetting realisation that I need Mr Kiss to say something, just so that I don't break down.

'You said your relationship with Sachi has been plagued with problems because of your blood type, right? How did you even realise you weren't compatible?'

'One winter night in Tokyo, I was trying to buy condoms from a vending machine, which asked for your blood type. Can you imagine how crazy that is? Anyway, that's when Sachi learned that my blood type is B+. I saw her face go pale, so I asked her what was going on. 'Is your blood type really B+?' she asked, I said it was,

68

but I didn't understand what bothered her so much at first. Back then I didn't know about the whole blood type theory. I learned later that in Japan, many think that B+ men are untrustworthy, especially when it comes to relationships. We're supposed to be egotistical and stubborn, and neglectful of our partner's desires. Tons of books and articles on that subject have been published in Japan and Korea. There have even been songs about it! It's made life a nightmare for a part of the male population.'

Mr Kiss and Sachi seem to be on a dead-end track, too, but it's not too late for them to find another way. There is still hope, depending on what Sachi's prepared to do for love. But she'll have to go against her family's beliefs and break with tradition if she wants this to work. If I were in her situation, I'm not sure I would have that courage.

7:56 pm

We're now Place de la Concorde, with its obelisk and monumental fountains – the Maritime Fountain to the south, and the Fountain of the Rivers to the north. It all looks so majestic, so perfect! The soft sound of water flowing grows ever louder as we get closer to the centre of the square.

I see Japanese couples, brides in long white dresses, and people surrounding them, taking pictures. Mr Kiss turns to me with a wistful smile. 'Sachi's dream is to get married right here,' he says, before changing the subject. 'She has a red Shiba Inu that her parents gave her for her twenty-first birthday. And he talks! He's the only one in her family who seems to like me a little.'

'What does Shiba Inu mean?'

'It means "little dog".'

'They must be easy to train.'

'Quite the opposite, actually. They're very independent, and they've got a mind of their own. They've lived in the mountains of Japan for a long, long time. They're said to be part dog, part man, part cat, and part monkey, and to have a deep soul.'

'What about Sachi's?'

'To me, he embodies love, fidelity, and respect. Sachi is devoted to Shiba, she even refused to come to Paris with me so she could stay with him. He's kind of a confidant to her, she tells him all her secrets. She always says that Shibas understand everything you tell them, and claims you can tell just by looking at their eyes. They share our trials and tribulations.'

Being far from Sachi can't be easy for Mr Kiss. Having to leave the people we love behind is always painful, but sometimes, having to abandon objects can have a similar effect. I felt almost physically sick the day I had to leave behind the some five thousand books I'd bought over the seven and a half years I studied history. Books were subsidised in East Germany and cost very little. I didn't have much money, but I used to spend almost all of it on books. Every once in a while I would even skip lunch or dinner so that I could afford a book. The East German government wanted to promote international culture and literature, and you could find most books you may have been looking for there.

When I left the country, I was already married, and Martín was back in Ecuador. I got in touch with an antique bookseller, and when I told him I needed money to join my husband, he offered to come to my apartment to make an estimation of how much my book collection might be worth. I needed eight thousand five hundred marks and was five thousand short, which, as luck would have it, was exactly the sum he offered.

'I had to find quite a lot of money to be able to leave my country,' I tell Mr Kiss as we wait for a light to turn green. 'Was it the same for you?'

'Yes. In order to flee Romania, I needed more than just courage. I knew people who would take care of everything for a hefty sum, but they asked for half the money up front, in order to pay for transportation and everything. The other half was due as soon as you'd crossed the border. If you were unlucky enough to get caught while trying to escape, any money you'd already paid was lost. A friend of mine left shortly before I did, and he sent me a postcard telling me he'd made it safely to the other side. So I went to see his brother and asked him to help me with my own escape plans. Others among my friends were arrested at the border, and I didn't hear from them again until after the regime fell. A few even got killed. Those of us who wanted freedom had to risk everything and hope for the best. But when you live under an authoritarian regime, sometimes the craving for freedom becomes such that you forget all about danger.'

I waited two and a half years to leave, trying to put aside as much money as I could, until finally I decided to sell my books. One might think that marrying someone from the West was a quick and easy way to get a passport and a work permit, but that wasn't the case at all. I had to file a ton of paperwork to make my marriage to Martín official and ask for the authorisation to follow him back to Ecuador, and even then, it actually made things more complicated.

Marrying someone from the West was indeed problematic. Everything had to be supervised by the state, including my trip to join him. Martín was one of thousands of foreigners studying in East German universities, and he never faced any difficulties while working towards his degree. But my filing a request to marry him precluded me from defending my thesis.

Every four or five months I would get an official-looking postcard asking me to come to some place or other to be subjected to what amounted to a police interrogation. I guess they wanted to make sure I was sincere and not a spy or something. They would ask the same questions over and over again, trying to trip me up and force me to contradict myself. The summons always came in the form of postcards, so that everyone knew who was under government surveillance. After a while I couldn't take it any more and did everything I could to leave as soon as they would let me.

The Pont de la Concorde is only about 160 yards long, but I could cross it a thousand times without ever experiencing the same sensation. The wind, the light, and the sounds of traffic always come together in different ways. If you've ever seen the Place de la Concorde in a rear-view mirror, you know what I'm talking about. The way light reflects off the Seine always seems to echo the city's mood. The light's always a different colour, too, from dark blue to metal grey, from ochre to crimson. I like trying to precisely identify what colour the light is every time I cross the bridge.

The wind whistles as it blows, as if it were trying to keep the passers-by company. Its sound mixes with the loud whir of the cars. I've always been weirdly fascinated by this bridge, perhaps simply because I have crossed it so many times in my life, be it on foot, on a motorcycle, in a car, or on a bus.

It's the first time since I got into this cab that I can feel the breeze off the Seine on my face, and smell its scent.

7:57 pm
We've both been silent for a few minutes now. Mr Kiss is as lost in his thoughts as I am, I can tell by looking at

him in the rear-view mirror. I feel a sort of anxiety whenever he seems to drift away like that, as if he were abandoning me. I try in vain to resist the urge to drag him back to the present.

'After Romania, Tokyo must have seemed like another planet.'

'You can say that again. It took me a while to adapt to the Japanese way of life. In fact, I think I only managed to do so thanks to Sachi. She straddles the gap between her country's traditions and aspirations for a way of life that's closer to what I'm used to. People in Tokyo live according to an extremely rigorous discipline, Sachi even more than most. Yet she's got a rebellious side, too, that comes through in the way she dresses. She's always had a knack for finding unique clothes in thrift stores and the like, and she loves to combine materials and colours you'd never think of wearing together. It never looks tacky on her, I don't know how she does it. It's like a challenge for her, as she was raised in a country where people traditionally favour simple clothes and muted colours. I think all this is a form of artistic experimentation for her, a way to go beyond what she's been taught in architecture school. She's very open-minded, always willing to try new things. She's the same way with music: she's a jazz-aficionado who seeks out records that are notoriously hard to get into, because of their originality or complexity. Her understanding of music is informed by architecture – or maybe it's the other way around – and she says she can hear geometrical shapes in the sound of certain instruments, see movements appearing before her eyes, like lines dividing space.

'She once compared her particular conception of music with the work of artist Fred Sandback, who uses interlocking threads and wires to delineate space in otherwise empty rooms.'

There's a short silence, then Mr Kiss picks up again. 'What do you do for a living, if you don't mind my asking?'

'I work for the German embassy. As a historian.'

Every new graduate in East Germany was offered a job by the authorities and the university. Those who refused, of course, were blacklisted, and had to look for another job on their own.

When I turned down the job I'd been offered as an editor for Dietz Verlag, which published communist propaganda, they made me sign a paper saying I didn't need the help of the university any more. I was suspect simply because I'd married someone from the West, and they wouldn't allow me to work as a historian. It was too much like espionage. There were opportunities for those who, like me, spoke other languages, though. For my thesis I'd worked on international fascism, which is why I'd been allowed to take language classes at the same time. My schedule was a nightmare, and I often had classes from 8:00 am to 8:00 pm.

The LDPD, or Liberal Democratic Party of Germany, was a party made up mostly of intellectuals. Thanks to my knowledge of English, French, and Spanish, I was hired as a translator, but I didn't work for them long. Soon enough I was leaving for Ecuador.

Single women were protected in East Germany, though. Young mothers were encouraged not to abandon their professional careers, and the many child-care centres allowed them to continue working, knowing that their children would be taken care of during the day. It was made as easy as possible for young women to hold onto their jobs. War caused economic disaster for East Germany, and everyone had to pitch in to rebuild the country. Meanwhile, West Germany was receiving economic help from the Americans as part of the Marshall Plan, which allowed the country to right the ship, economically speaking within the decade that followed the end of the war.

The deutschemark, the West German currency, was worth much more than its East German counterpart, and was therefore sought after even in the East. We used to call it the 'Westgeld,' or Western Gold. Soon stores called Intershops started appearing in the East. There you could buy rare and expensive products with deutsche-marks, generally obtained from tourists who came from the West. Twenty deutschemarks were worth about a hundred of our East German marks.

Whenever friends from the West visited, I would wait for them at Checkpoint Charlie with butterflies in my stomach, imagining all the things they might be bringing us. Chocolate was what I always hoped for. Others would hope for books or newspapers, but those were harder to sneak in. People would often hide *Der Spiegel* – 'the magazine of choice for Western intellectuals', as we called it – under their clothes, flattening the pages against their body in the hope that the customs officers wouldn't notice anything.

Even today I have to pinch myself sometimes, to make sure it really is all over. No one would have thought that possible back then.

The days and nights that directly followed the fall of the Wall are historic moments filled with emotions for a people who found themselves free almost overnight. All of a sudden Berlin got a second wind and seemed to regain its former splendour, in spite of the scars the war had left everywhere, the ruined facades and the walls riddled with bullet holes. You can't walk through the city without thinking of all the pain it's had to endure. It's still all there, and it's quite moving.

'I miss Berlin,' I say all of a sudden. 'I miss feeling so close to history, feeling it nourish me. Do you know what I mean?'

'I think I do, yes. But it's a little different in Romania. We suffered for so long under the rule of one cruel figure that that sense of belonging to a larger history sort of disappeared, because all our hate was focused on Ceausescu and his evil cohorts.'

'I guess that's the major difference between our countries. Your oppressor wasn't an entire system, but a human dictator. I can see how that would give history a more bitter taste, and make it harder to deal with.'

'In the last moments before the execution of Ceausescu in December 1989, you could feel the hatred the entire country had for him. I don't think it ever was like that in East Germany. Freedom came not with executions, but progressively, as the Communist regime got weaker and weaker until it lost even its *raison d'être*.'

'It seems a lot of us feel like exiles. I mean, sometimes we are, like you in Paris, in Japan, or in Canada, but isn't that how you feel in Romania, too, in a way? And what about Sachi, who doesn't feel entirely at home in Japan? As for me, well, my country doesn't even exist any more! I think we're becoming more and more rootless.'

'That's what connects us, you and me. This feeling of being rootless. I don't think it's something that's limited to one particular country.'

'I guess I understand you better than would one of your countrymen who'd never left Romania.'

'You'd think that with all those people moving across borders, racism and xenophobia would be on the decline, but they're actually even more prevalent than before. Perhaps it even contributes to that, who knows?'

'I know what you mean. It's paradoxical, too, because some people actually feel more at home in countries other than their own. I came across an example not so long ago, riding the Eurostar from London to Paris. It's actually quite a story.'

'What happened, if you don't mind my asking.'

'Not at all. Well, I was standing in the aisle of my compartment, waiting for the person next to me to sit down. That's when I saw this elderly gentleman, an elegant Englishman with a fedora and a cane. He looked like a real English dandy. He came right up to me and asked me to show him his seat, having obviously mistaken me for an employee of the train company. I asked him to show me his ticket so I could help him, and it turned out he was sitting right behind me, by the window. As we were talking, a young Englishman got on and sat on the seat right next to me. He took his laptop out and started working, or pretending to work. As soon as the train had left, the dandy started singing French songs, without any hint of an accent. This prompted my neighbour to pick up his laptop and go sit a little further down the car. Now that the seat was no longer taken, the dandy came to sit beside me. He spent the entire trip telling me all about his life while ordering bottle after bottle of red wine. He was Irish and spoke French fluently. Thirty minutes later he'd already invited me to come spend some time in his house in Sicily. "When you get to Taormina," he said, "just asked for Don Camilo and they'll direct you to my house."

'His story soon became surreal. He told me his mother had been a writer, and he was travelling from country to country to collect royalties. He told me her name was Pamela Lyndon, and she'd created Mary Poppins. I glanced at my former neighbour who'd been eavesdropping for a while, but he didn't seem impressed at all. Anyway, the point is that the son of Mrs. Mary Poppins's creator feels at home in Sicily and not at all among the English, with whom he supposedly shares more cultural baggage.'

'Yes, that's exactly what you were saying.'

'Forgive me if I'm being rude, but why did you leave Japan when Sachi is still there? Did you feel like you couldn't fit in there?'

'That wasn't really the problem. I think I can fit in pretty much anywhere, really. It's just that with all that blood type nonsense, I felt that the only people who could help me were my French saviours. I still consider them my adoptive family, and when I didn't know what to do, I turned to them once again. I wrote them and explained the situation as well as I could. They did not understand right away, but really, who could blame them? This whole thing would make no sense to most Europeans.

'Sachi and I were at a loss for what to do to overcome this obstacle, but they knew how to make me feel better. They told me not to give up hope and said they'd do their best to help me solve what they called "this Japanese puzzle".

'That's why I came back to Paris, to try to find a solution. I thought perhaps I could change my blood type here, or something.'

'I see. I'll ask my husband about it, he should be able to give you the number of someone at the Institut Pasteur who might be able to help you, or at least to answer your questions.'

'Thank you so much. Remind me to give you my information before you go.'

An impossible love, the weight of family tradition, and the cruelty of injustice. I know all too well what he is going through.

If you walk the streets of Berlin in the winter, you'll only ever see people's eyes and noses, because of all the layers of clothes they have to wear to protect themselves against the freezing cold. Back then the temperature would often drop to -15°C in the winter. One time, as we were walking around the Weihnachtsmarkt, the Christmas market by the Nikolaikirche, we stopped in front of a small kiosk that sold records from the '20s and other original recordings. In spite of the cold, we stayed there, listening to the melodies and words of all those old German and English songs. He was like a child, so excited to have me discover all those treasures.

'There's something I want to tell you,' he said.

'What is it?'

'I dream of us moving in together.'

I've never forgotten that scene. He and I, standing in the middle of the snow-covered market, frozen to the bone but happy as can be. I remember it as if it were yesterday.

This time Mr Kiss picks up where we left off of his own accord. Maybe he's starting to notice how uncomfortable I get whenever he remains quiet for too long.

'We visited most of the temples in Tokyo and Kyoto,

Sachi and I,' he says. 'She finds the purity of their architecture fascinating, so whenever we were on a get-away together, we'd make it a point to visit one of those places of emotion and silence. There's a Swiss architect who says he finds inspiration in the purity of temples and in their relationship to nature, and who tries to work according to what he calls an "emotional understanding of space". He focuses on the atmosphere a building creates, because he believes that's where its eventual perfection will come from.

'Anyway, I would get away from my workshop and she would leave her precious books to join me. We'd always meet in a different place to visit a new holy site.

'One day, as we were on our way to the Sinnyodo monastery, I stopped suddenly, as if I'd just been hit by lightning. I took her by the hand and led her to a small doorway a little uphill from the temple, the entrance to a dark and mysterious alley. I hugged her tight and told her, our lives were really beginning now, right there. The doorway was a symbol of our new start together. The alley was lined with bamboo trees, nature's way of telling us that our path would not be without obstacles. Her reaction was not what I expected. She didn't seem to know what to say, and the joy I could see in her eyes soon gave way to a sadness I'd never seen before. Then I remembered her asking me about my blood type, and I understood then that if we wanted to have a future together, we needed to solve that problem. We hadn't talked about it until that moment.'

8:00 pm

The trees that line the Boulevard Saint-Germain let through a soft light that bathes the cars and passers-by. The rays of sunlight seem to pierce the green leaves and, along with the shadows projected by the buildings, create a sort of chiaroscuro.

My phone is ringing again. I see it's my daughter, and before she has time to say anything, I say, 'I'm running a little late, but don't worry, we'll do some last-minute shopping as soon as I get there. Then we should have more than enough time to put the finishing touches on the dinner.'

'Great. Send me a text when you're close and I'll come down.'

'If we don't hit traffic again, I should be home in about twenty minutes. I hope the bakery's still open, I'd like to pick up shortbread biscuits and apple tarts.'

While I'm talking to my daughter, I look at Mr Kiss more closely. A leather bracelet festooned with a silver square-shaped ring catches my eye.

I don't particularly like jewellery on men, but this particular piece is discreet, not gaudy at all. I hadn't noticed it up until now, partly because he wears it on his left wrist.

'I really like your bracelet,' I say after hanging up.

'Thank you.'

'Mind if I ask where you got it?'

'It was a gift from Sophie, you know, the young woman I saved from drowning. I don't know where she bought it, though.'

I can see this is still an emotional subject for him, so I decide not to push it. If he wants to say more, it's up to him. But he remains quiet.

My tenor used to wear a piece of jewellery, too, a thick signet ring with ancient engravings. I can still feel the cold of it on my skin and lips. Sometimes it would dig into my flesh painfully, but I never asked him to take it off. It was like a fetish to him.

When I first arrived in Paris, I used to stare hungrily at everything, especially the stalls of the fresh fruit sellers at the market, with their colourful and appetising products. Out-of-season was rare and expensive in East Germany. You couldn't find cherries or strawberries in the winter, and you could forget about exotic fruits altogether. Here, though, any craving can be satisfied at any time. One thing we did have was meat, which was pretty cheap at that. Fish, though, was rare. Most people had their own garden and grew what base crops they could.

8:01 pm

I've always found the Boulevard Saint-Germain fascinating, with its many illustrious residents. Guillaume Apollinaire, André Malraux, and Edouard Branly, all lived behind the doors we're passing right now, and Charles Baudelaire and Alfred de Musset were even born here! I imagine history coming to life before my eyes in the form of these old stone buildings.

'Do you have any idea just how many historical figures have lived on this Boulevard?' I ask Mr Kiss.

'Yes, I always think about that when I'm here. You know, Bucharest too was a buzzing intellectual centre, for a while. Paris and Bucharest have a lot in common, actually. Many artists of the European avant-garde were originally from Romania. People like Tristan Tzara, Victor Brauner, or Marcel Janco. Camil Petrescu, too, and Constantin Brancusi, of course. They all lived in Bucharest, at least for a while. They'd meet in coffee shops, much like Sartre and de Beauvoir here. The Enach Diu café in Bucharest is kind of our Deux Magots or Flore café, really. The early twentieth century saw a lot of exchange between French and Romanian artists, too. Brancusi and Duchamp, for instance, fed off each other a lot. All those artists would meet during exhibitions and cocktail parties.

'Perhaps that's why I feel at home in Paris,' he adds.

'You're right. I wish I could have lived back then.'

8:04 pm

A man on the sidewalk catches my eye. He's talking to a woman with exaggerated hand motions and expressions that remind me of Louis de Funès. The first time I saw one of his movies was in East Germany. Those were translated in the West, then shown during the Sommer-kino, a summer film festival. They showed avant-garde films, many of which had strong political overtones, and art films from France, Italy, Spain, or even the United States. A ticket cost almost nothing back then.

The German film industry wasn't thriving after the war, on both sides of the Wall. I remember one particular movie called *Die Heiden von Kummerow und ihre lustigen Streichen*, or *The Heathens of Kummerow*. Based on a novel by Ehm Welk and directed by Werner Jacobs, it came out in 1967. It's about a group of young Germans living in a small town, about their games and struggles, and their relationships with adults. We follow them as they outgrow their Christian upbringing and develop a rather revolutionary class consciousness. The film had had a great impact on me at the time.

'I have to admit I didn't feel at home right away when I first got to Tokyo,' Mr Kiss says. 'I was aware of the huge gap that exists between their culture and mine. One time, after we'd spent the night drinking and singing karaoke, Sachi and I ended up in one of Tokyo's many love hotels. I was so drunk I didn't notice how sordid a place it was. All I can remember is going through the cupboards in the bathroom. In a drawer I found a pack of condoms, but apparently those weren't made for people with a specific blood type. Those are weird places, where eroticism seems always to be on sale. That made me more than a little uncomfortable. Have you seen Sofia Coppola's *Lost in Translation*?'

'Several times, actually.'

'I find it to be a very accurate description of the way circumstances sometimes make it almost impossible to express one's feelings.'

'Almost nothing happens, but the stakes are very high.'

'There's a kind of cerebral eroticism running all through it, something that never quite becomes words. We see the questions in their eyes, but we don't know exactly what those are. I've always felt like an alien in Japan. People there always act withdrawn and overly formal, and I don't know why, but it also changes you.'

'It must be hard to actually become close to people there.'

'I tried for a long while with Sachi's family, but they're not the most open-minded people, to put it mildly.'

'The contrast between you must be huge.'

'It is. They're very complex people, though. For instance, I know they admire the work of a Japanese photographer named Araki. He takes erotic pictures of very young girls in suggestive, borderline pornographic poses. Modesty's a core value of the traditions they hold so dear, yet at the same time they don't seem to have a problem with objectifying women that way. There's a cognitive dissonance there I just can't understand.'

It's strange how we always feel the need to try and fit the way other people think within our own world-view. Wouldn't it be easier if we just accepted that, sometimes, we simply can't understand? It was my tenor who actually gave me the answer to that question, and many others: 'Remember the subtitle to *Thus Spoke Zarathustra*, "*Ein Buch für Alle und Keinen*". A book for all and none.' I think of that title every time I have to deal with people whose attitude or way of thinking I can't understand.

'Sachi helped me get over that feeling of uneasiness that threatened to overwhelm me in Tokyo,' Mr Kiss says. 'With her help, I was able to focus on the many things the city has to offer. We would often take a walk together at night, exploring the city's back alleys and letting Tokyo's smells and colours wash over us. That's how I discovered another aspect of traditional Japan, one you can't see in broad daylight. Like a hidden truth that revealed itself to me and guided me through an ancient culture I thought had disappeared.

'I particularly remember the smell of public bath houses. My studio flat didn't have a bathroom, but there was a communal one in the hallway. You had to pay to use the shower, though, and at 100 yens the five minutes, it soon became ruinous. Then I discovered public bath houses, where you can stay for as long as you want for only 170 yens, and it changed my life. The public baths are called "sento", I learned, and monks used to be frequent visitors.

'Part of the appeal of those places, I came to understand, is the ritual you have to go through every time. First they make you go into a changing room, where you take off your shoes and put them in a locker. Then you take off all your clothes, soap yourself up while sitting on a wooden stool in front of a mirror, and take a short shower. Only then are you allowed to enter the hot bath –

slowly of course, given that the water is usually kept at a temperature between 40 and 50°. And when you get out, you take another shower. The baths used to be segregated by gender, then they were made unisex again. Nowadays there's usually a two-meter-high wall separating men and women.

'I tried to learn Japanese, but then Sachi decided she would be my teacher. She didn't care about teaching me the basics, words that would have been useful in my everyday life. What she wanted, though, was to help me feel the poetry of her language, its images, its philosophy. So I learned words like *asu-ka*, which means the smell of the morning, or *hon*, which is both the root and the beginning. And things like *yokan*, too, which is the name they give those delicious red bean pastries.

'Instead of a dictionary, she gave me a book, Jun'ichirō Tanizaki's *The Tattooer*. He was only twenty-four when he wrote it and had it published in a magazine, in 1910. It's a cruel and cynical story, which came as a shock to many at the time. That's why Sachi was fascinated by it, though. She likes to push limits and challenge the establishment and its morals.

'One day, she insisted that I come with her see a kabuki play. She said that artists could learn a lot by trying to understand the essence of Japanese philosophy and its expression in everyday life as well as in the arts.'

'I think darkness plays as important a role as light in theatre,' I say. 'Don't you?'

'Indeed. There's one scene in particular that comes to

mind: a glossy wooden floor, pillars and screens casting shadows on the stage, and a darkness suddenly descending from the sky on an actor, as if to smother him.'

'I can imagine the effect that might have, yes. Many artists nowadays focus on the way lighting interacts with their work. Take Robert Wilson, for instance.'

'The Texan director? I often see posters for his shows when I drive by the Châtelet or Bastille.'

'Do you know how he started out?'

'Not at all. How?'

'He introduced his first piece at the Shiraz art festival, in Iran. It took place over seven days in the desert. The audience was supposed to walk from one dune to the next – I think there were seven in total, too – to follow the path of light from dawn to sundown and, eventually, complete darkness.'

'That sounds very poetic indeed. When was that?'

'In the early '70s, I think.'

'I'll mention it to Sachi, she'll no doubt find it inspiring. I'll try to take her to see his work the next time she's in Paris, too.'

We stay silent for a moment, then I hear him whisper, ' "Our blood must not come between us. I'll find a solution, I promise you." That's what she told me. I can't ever forget those words, but now I'm the one who has to find a solution.'

One night he played something I'd never heard before.

'Guess who wrote this piece,' he said.

I came up with five names, five wrong answers.

'It's not easy, I'll give you that. I'm not sure I would have figured it out, either, so I'll give you a hint. He wrote this piece when he was fourteen. He loved music, but he loved words and thoughts even more, so in the end he let others play with notes and bars.'

'I have no idea who that could be.'

'And he's German.'

'East or West?'

'I'll give you a quote, maybe it'll help.'

'I doubt it, but go ahead.'

' "*Die Einen reisen, weil sie sich suchen; die Andered, weil sie sich verlieren möchten.*" You must have read that before.'

'OK, I give up.'

'Nietzsche!'

'Really? I had no idea he started out as a composer!'

'Yes, Nietzsche! And speaking of him, I'd love to visit Sils-Maria with you, that town in Switzerland where he used to spend the summer.'

Thinking about my passion for him and its consequences still upsets me, even two decades later. How could that be? Perhaps I was naïve to think that time would help. Instead, my feelings have burrowed deep inside me, so deep that neither the passage of time nor the greatest efforts of will would allow me to heal. Perhaps it isn't all over, as I thought it was. Mr Kiss's determination may be what's rekindling this hope inside me. Love is a treasure that must be protected at all cost. We may always have to face our pain and disappointment alone, but sometimes, an outside help can prove miraculous.

I realise now I've never really said Auf Wiedersehen to him. If I'd had Mr Kiss's courage, I would have gone looking for him instead of giving up.

8:06 pm

The intense August light still warms my shoulder through the open window of the cab. I take off my sunglasses and let the light bathe me completely. The sky won't change colour for another hour, when it'll turn to shades of orange and fuchsia. Back in East Germany, I never knew such light. The sun there didn't seem to give off heat, but to be a cold star.

I always feel like I'm experiencing the reality of History when I go to places where you could see the Wall when it still stood, like by the Engelbecken, the 'Angel's Pool', right at the border between the two German states. There's a Bauhaus building designed by Max and Bruno Taut that used to serve as headquarters for the Party's *Jugend* there, at the corner of the Engeldamm Strasse.

There's also the Saint Michael church, one of Berlin's oldest Catholic churches, which sits between the Mitte and Kreuzberg neighbourhoods, by the Luisenkanal. It used to be one of our favourite hangouts. It's in that very church that we once listened to the adagio from Mahler's *Symphony No. 5*. I remember how I'd closed my eyes and let the music carry me to faraway lands, far from Berlin and its Wall. How could I have known that some day I would find myself on the other side of the Wall, forever separated from the man who'd taught me all about love?

Thinking back on those moments of happiness is painful, but at the same time, the feelings of incompleteness they trigger force me to look within myself, to realise that the time may have come to go back and try to re-establish that link with my past I'd so carelessly broken.

Plazas, streets, bridges, alleys, avenues, they all seem to call your name, to tattoo it on my face.

8:07 pm

Mr Kiss is silent again, but I am longing for him to continue his story. I want to let his words carry me like a river, hoping they'll guide me to a shore I never knew existed.

'Sorry to keep changing the subject, but how's life in Romania now?' I say. 'It must have improved considerably since the fall of Ceausescu, right?'

'Yes, things are much better, especially now that the country's entered the EU. Many associations have also been created to help the poor. In fact, my adoptive family has its own project there. They're trying to help street orphans, many of whom do drugs or sniff glue. They bought a house just outside Bucharest and they're working with a priest who's been an invaluable help with the kids. Their goal is to get the children to come to the centre to get them clean and sober, and then to help them find a place in society. They're working with a team of

Romanian volunteers who specialise in helping drug abusers. In the long run, they're hoping that the children they're helping will be able to re-enter the system and find a job that allows them to thrive. Those people really are heroes. Their kindness and dedication help give my people hope, and God knows that's something we need.'

'That's very generous of them. But I guess it's also their way of paying back what Romania gave them, don't you think?'

'Yes, you're probably right.'

On the other side of the Iron Curtain, in Romania like in East Germany, nobody could be trusted. I was taught to always be careful about what I was saying, even among friends or at home. That was just the way it was. There was no way to know who may have been working for the secret police.

What does Mr Kiss feel when he looks back on his past life? I lean forward between the two front seats and say, 'Have you been able to forget the past? I mean, can you look back on it without feeling bitter or nostalgic?'

'Yes. I left it all behind the minute I crossed the border, really. That moment was so fantastic that the rest kind of faded away, leaving only the best memories.'

'I thought I'd managed to let go of everything that had caused me pain, too. But now I realise that's not the case at all, that I still have to face some feelings I'd repressed. I still have quite a bit of work to do on that front.'

'We all work through those issues at our own pace. We can't all expect to let go of the past at the exact same moment. And it's not all up to you, either. There are a lot of things that can get in the way.'

'I guess, but talking about it can help. It can be therapeutic, as they say. I think that's what I've been missing. I was never brave enough to face those painful memories head-on. Instead I let them fester for much too long.'

'Suffering's not that different from everything else in life, really. You've got to learn how to do it.'

8:09 pm

We've finally reached the Boulevard Raspail. It's only a one-lane street here, but thankfully taxis are allowed to use bus lanes, so we dodge most of the traffic.

Every time I'm on this boulevard, I can't help but think I could have run into Aragon here, like a friend of mine did. We'd known each other since high school and when he left Germany for Paris, I'd given him a book of Persian poetry by Omar Khayyâm. One day he was walking down the boulevard with that very book under his arm when, coming from the rue de Varenne, there was Aragon. He walked up to him and asked if he would be willing to sign his book. Years later, when we met again here in Paris, my friend told me that story and proudly showed me the signed book.

I've always been fascinated by the admiration artists provoke, and how they can spark inspiration in their admirers. France has always been a destination of choice for foreign students, including young men and women from Japan eager to study fine arts. It must be like fulfilling a dream to land in the country of Cézanne, Matisse, Braque, or Picasso. The Provence countryside has always been a large source of inspiration, and young painters often start off by trying to imitate Cézanne.

But as they grow older and more experienced, artists tend to develop their own language. Take, for instance, Vong Phaophanit, who came to France from Laos and who started out the exact same way. His goal was to break through the purely visual dimension of his art to get to the essence of things. According to him, our understanding of the world is remade each day, based on both our past circumstances and the path we want to follow going forward.

What I'm getting at is, I guess, that there's a sort of mutability, an inherent ability to evolve in the images we come across, and in those we create. At any time, these images can shift and let us glimpse something else, some new meaning we didn't know was there. What is it that we see, really? Don't even familiar things possess a hidden dimension we can only guess or imagine?

Isn't that how we interact with objects from before our time, too? When faced with something even just a hundred years old, what we perceive first is its presence in the now, its relative place in time.

8:10 pm

I really should focus on what I need to do before our guests arrive. No need to unpack my suitcases: that can wait. I'll just leave them in my room and take care of them tomorrow. What matters is that everything is right in the living room. That means the tables, flowers, and cocktails.

I reach into my pocket, looking for the gum I bought at Athens airport, but pull out a box of matches instead. I collect matches from all the bars, cafés, and restaurants I go to. It's my way of remembering those places. Each box is unique, as it bears the name of the place it came from. Some are even little works of art. And they're quite useful, too. Back before technology allowed us to magically find everything just by moving our index finger around on a screen, those boxes were like miniature phonebooks. I used to have a whole lot of them, back in East Germany, but when I moved to Ecuador, and then to Paris, I had to leave them behind. I still pick them up whenever I discover a new place, though; I never managed to shake off the habit. This one's from a tiny restaurant on Hydra, an island in Greece, where I had dinner a few days ago. It's a very simple box of a deep blue colour.

Of course, if I'm being honest, my being a smoker is now the main reason why I still pick those up wherever I go.

'I love those matchboxes you find in bars,' I say. 'Do you smoke, Mr Kiss?'

'No. When I was young, in Romania, we would write

messages in code inside those boxes, and we would pass them around. That way no one else knew what we were up to.'

'The first time I met my husband in college, I asked him for a light.'

'And he offered you matches?'

'No, actually, he wasn't a smoker. But he moved heaven and earth just to find me a light. I think that's what first impressed me about him, that sense of dedication. Speaking of which, if you do find a solution to your problem, how do you picture your future with Sachi?'

'We've talked about it a lot already. As soon as she's done with college, we're planning on settling down together here, in France. She shouldn't have too much trouble finding a job here, my friends have contacts in architecture firms all over the country. As for me, I can't work pretty much anywhere, so I wouldn't mind moving to another city if we have to.'

'A few of my friends are architects. I know they tend to favour a minimalist style. They'll probably be interested in working with a young architect trained in Japan. I'd be happy to get you in touch with them.'

'That's very nice of you, we would be very grateful. If you don't mind, I'll contact you as soon as she gets here.'

'Of course. Say, is religion also a problem in your relationship?'

'Not really. We can work things out on that front.'

'So your blood is the only problem?'

'Yes. Unfortunately, I don't know how we can over-come it.'

'I can't wait to find out more about this. I'll let you know, of course.'

'Thank you so much again. You know, I always carry the letter Sachi's father wrote me. It's heart rending. I couldn't even bring myself to show it to her. It would hurt her too much to know.'

We stop at a red light, and Mr Kiss takes a notebook out of his briefcase. Inside it is the letter. He hands it to me, and in his eyes I think I can see both trust and expectation.

I take it gingerly and reach into my bag for my glasses. The letter is short and in simple English, and it goes straight to the point.

Dear Mister Kiss,

My family and I have been made aware of your relationship with Sachi. Traditions and customs are very important to us. Up until now, all the members of our family have respected those basic rules.

We do not object to relationships with persons of different religions, or from other countries. After all, the world is one big, unified place now.

Here's why I'm writing to you today: while we have a lot of respect for those who are different from us, there is one thing we cannot accept. You know what I'm referring to. We do not wish for B+ blood to mix with ours.

I found it impossible to say this to you directly, which is why I decided to write to you. I hope that you will understand our family's concerns and respect our beliefs.

Sincerely yours,

Yoji Harumi

This is just as heart rending as Mr Kiss said it was. I can't stop my hands from shaking as I read.

8:16 pm

'I don't know what to say, Mr Kiss. It's so unfair.'

I hand him back the letter. He seems to think about what I've just said for a moment.

'You know,' he finally says, 'in times of hardship such as these, I always think back on what my father taught me. He's had a long and rich life, and he's also an avid reader. He used to work in the fields, he loves being surrounded by nature. He's a very wise man. He seems to always have a quote at the ready from one of the many books he's read, and it always seems to apply to your current situation, whatever it is.'

'Is he still with us?'

'He is. Ninety years old, and still completely lucid. He still knows by heart things he read half a century ago.'

'I hope I'm the same when I'm ninety!'

'He told me a story recently, one he read in a collection written by Jorge Luis Borges. A short story called "The Disk". Have you read it?'

'No, it doesn't ring a bell.'

'Well, it's about a one-sided disk, called the Disk of Odin. One night, an elderly man, wrapped in an old raggedy blanket, comes knocking on a woodcutter's door. He walks slowly and with a cane. He asks the woodcutter if he could stay here for the night, as he's been walking across all of England and doesn't have a place to stay. The woodcutter lets him in, and they share a silent dinner. The next morning, they set out together. The path is covered in snow. Suddenly the old man drops his cane, and asks the woodcutter to pick it up for him. The woodcutter, surprised, asks why he should obey. The old man replies that he is a king and, in order to prove it, he offers to let him touch the palm of his hand, which he's kept firmly closed up until now. The woodcutter is understandably taken aback, but he eventually agrees to touch the old man's palm. There's something cold in the old man's hand, and the woodcutter thinks he sees like a flash of light, but before he can see more, the old man closes his hand again.'

'What was it? Was there actually something in his hand to begin with?'

'Oh yes, there was. The old man then proceeds to explain that what the woodcutter felt was a one-sided disk, a literally unique item, and that as long as it remains in his possession, he will remain king. The woodcutter wants to know if the disk is made of gold. He can already picture himself acquiring the disk and becoming a king. So he offers to buy the disk for a few gold coins.'

'I imagine the king refused.'

'Of course.'

'What happened then?'

'Well, then the woodcutter hits the old man over the head and kills him, and the disk falls on the ground. The woodcutter goes into the woods to dispose of the body, but when he comes back, he's unable to find the disk, which fell with its invisible side up. He spends the rest of his life looking for it, but never finds it.'

'Talk about a cautionary tale about greed and dissatisfaction ... '

'It's one of my favourite stories. It taught me that I should be happy with what I have and what I can earn thanks to my work. Sometimes, when I feel like my life has become unbearable and I wish I could speed things along, I think about that story, and I say to myself, "Just enjoy what you have. All in good time." '

That's the moment my phone chooses to start ringing. It's my daughter again. It's getting late.

'Yes, honey, I'm on my way. (...) Sure, an Opera cake, that sounds great. I'll take care of the rest of the dessert. I'm right by the Rue du Cherche-Midi. Do we have candles for the cake? (...) Great, then I'll just stop by the bakery to pick up the tarts. See you in a bit.'

'I'll try to find a less congested street,' Mr Kiss says after I hang up.

8:18 pm

The whole street seems to smell of Poilâne's fresh bread and apple tarts. There's a line, of course. We'll have to wait a little longer than I thought, but since I'm already running late … The street's very narrow, too, Mr Kiss won't be able to stop in front of the bakery.

'I don't know where I'll find a parking spot to wait for you,' he says.

'Don't worry about it. You can just drive a little ahead, and I'll find you.'

I leap out of the car, leaving my bag on the backseat. I've got some money in my pocket, along with my phone. As I'm waiting in line at the bakery, I can't help but think back on everything Mr Kiss and I just said to each other. I don't usually think about East Germany, about my mother and I moving there, about my love affair with my tenor. About the baby that I gave up on. Sometimes it feels as if someone else lived through it, and just told me about it.

I know it's sad, but I've deliberately broken off all ties with that period of my life, and anything that could remind me of it. I started a new life when I moved to Quito and found a job at the German embassy, then another when we came back to Europe and to France. Of the three stages of my life, the first one may have been the most important in the construction of my identity as a person, but it's the one I've tried to erase so desperately. Today's the first time I've ever faced that truth, tried to talk about it. Just by listening to a stranger's story, by trying to help him, I have unwittingly dived right back into that most important part of my life, without realising at once what we were saying really meant.

It's as if a switch inside me had been turned on. I opened my heart unexpectedly and, thinking back on it, I'm astonished that I was willing to talk so openly about my past and the traumas it caused with a perfect stranger. I take it as a sign that things have to change now. The only way I can be happy in the present is by accepting my past. I can begin a new chapter in my life without necessarily having to forget what came before.

What if I tried to find him now? He would remember me as a young woman, a young woman so different from the person I've become. But should I be afraid to show myself to someone I've loved so much in a different light, at a different stage in my life? Inside, at the core, I'm the same. Why should I be afraid of seeing him again? It's such a childish reaction.

I want to go back and break the thread that led to our separation. You used to look at me with that benevolent smile of yours, that smile that said you understood everything but still liked being surprised. I think I'm ready. I want to find you again, Jonas, I want to know again that happiness we shared, because I know it is still there, intact, deep inside me.

8:27 pm

As I come out of the bakery, Mr Kiss honks his horn from a little further up the street. I climb back into the taxi, and we're off again.

'I've really enjoyed talking with you, Mr Kiss, and I'm so glad to have met you. For once I really don't mind the trip took a little longer than expected.'

'It was my pleasure. You know, I don't go around telling every one of my passengers my life story. But I'm glad to have shared this experience with you.'

'I'm honoured. Do you ever feel like you'd want to run into some of your passengers again?'

'Yes, sometimes. There was that one lady who told me all about her life in fifteen minutes, and whom I've never seen again. She was originally from Iran but had moved to the United States, where she'd married a rich man. She told me a story about her youngest son, a real tragedy. They used to spend the summer on the French Riviera together. The summer he turned eighteen, he fell in love with a local girl, and they decided to move in together in a small apartment, not too far from Nice. He never went back to the US. He and his girlfriend were murdered in their home by a gang. She did all she could to help the police find the murderers, but to no avail. I met her as she was on her way back to the United States after months of working with the police. She said her son and his girlfriend never had a chance; apparently, they were the victims of a vendetta between the gang and the girl's family. She thought the murderers had friends in high places, too, people protecting them from the investigation.

'She decided to give up and withdraw from the world. She told me her life had lost its meaning, that she was going to retire to a faraway island, where she would know no one and no one would know her. Her story broke my heart. I wanted to help her so much. I hope I get to see her again some day. It's as if her fate had already been decided, and no one could have changed anything about it. I often wonder what happened to her. That was years ago, but I still think about her and her son. There are stories like that, true stories, which deeply affect even those who only hear them. Sometimes when I'm alone with Sachi, I feel this unexplainable fear grips me. And often when I'm waiting at the airport to pick up passengers arriving from across the ocean, I think I can see that poor woman's face looking at me in the crowd, and I can't help but hope she'll be the one to open the door and get into my cab. I wish I knew how she's doing. I was thinking about her again this morning.'

8:30 pm

We're almost there. As we drive by the Fondation Cartier, I ask Mr Kiss if he can slow down a little, so I can see what they're currently showing. Something about Amazonian Indians, it seems.

'The garden wall above the entrance is a perfect fit, then,' Mr Kiss says. 'Sachi knows this place pretty well, actually. They often show Japanese artists.

'One day, Sachi told me she had a surprise for me. She led me to a garden known for the many plants it houses. What fascinates her the most about flowers is all their different shapes and colours. We walked around for a few minutes, before stopping in front of a tree. In the fall, that tree seems to be ablaze with colours. Shades of gold, yellow, orange, red, even light green. Its branches spread out, forming like a shelter, but its leaves are delicate and fragile, like chiselled stone. If you stand under it, you can see the sky through the branches, and space turns into a canvas on which the leaves are like trails of paint. Sachi asked me if I knew what the name of the tree was.

'I'm not very good when it comes to plant names, even though I often use them as models for my tattoos. Their shapes inspire me. I always use that book of black and white photographs by Karl Blossfeldt, a German photographer from the early twentieth century. It's a great source of inspiration. He was also a sculptor, and used leaves to decorate his statues.

'Anyway, Sachi told me the tree was a Japanese maple tree, and that its name in English was "bloodgood". I remember how she smiled sadly at me when she said that.

'Now every time I see a Japanese maple, I tell myself it is a symbol of our love. Seems like I can't ever escape this whole blood thing. Even trees make me think about it. Who knew that one day, I'd be so obsessed with my blood type ... '

'Well, I can see why you would be.'

It is strange, though. Now that I think about it, I don't even know the blood types of my children.

8:31 pm

Last red light. I send Elinor a text, telling her to come down.

I feel like I've spent the past two hours travelling through time and space, to the corners of our lives and the depths of our souls. Sometimes an hour can mean more to us than several years. As we draw nearer to our destination, I once again go over my entire conversation with Mr Kiss, and realise I've unearthed a number of truths I'd never dared face before.

I feel stronger for having faced those memories. I know now that those moments of happiness I may have known at a certain point in my life haven't completely disappeared. On the contrary, they're still intact within me. I can summon them up in my mind, see and hear them again, relive them again, as intense as on the very first day.

Strangely, I remember that back then, when I was actually experiencing those moments for the first time, I could never shake off a little voice inside me that told me to enjoy them as much as I could. 'Relish these innocent times,' it seemed to say, 'so that you'll remember them forever as the best time of your life.'

Mr Kiss has helped me free my mind and bring all those memories back. It's like Nabokov writes in *Ada*; intense feelings such as these can remain dormant for a long, long time, waiting for the moment you'll be facing the object of your love again, or be put in a situation that reminds you of them. And when that happens, it's as if you were right back at the beginning, and those feelings are back, as if by magic.

It's a little as if you could buy stock in happiness, except it never loses its value. It would even tend to become more and more valuable as happiness becomes harder to come by. That's the way the market works, isn't it? Mr Kiss has taken a similar gamble on the future, except he's always been aware of it, unlike me. He's not afraid of his feelings, they're a source of inner strength for him. He doesn't even hesitate to share them with a total stranger. How kind and generous of him! I truly admire him.

We're both silent, both lost in thought. We're not paying attention to the sounds of the city any more. I feel so comfortable, at peace. It's been a long time since I've been aware of the silence like this. It's a silence full of meaning, a silence that knows it's accomplished its mission. It fills me completely, I can almost feel it. I have no desire to break it.

What is the meaning of my encounter with Mr Kiss? I think we both got something out of it, both learned something about ourselves. The road we have travelled together is more than just the distance between the airport and my house. No one's ever taken me so far. From our respective home countries, to the bottoms of our hearts; yes, that's the trip we just made together. And it won't be without consequences for our respective lives. I believe things happen for a reason.

I write down my name and phone number on a piece of paper, and give it to him.

'Here's my number. You can call me whenever you like. I'll talk to my husband about your problems. I can't promise you anything, but you're talking to the right person. I'll keep you posted.'

'I don't know what to say. I guess our fate is in your hands now. I'm sorry, I shouldn't say that. I don't want you to put any kind of pressure on you. I just meant – '

'I know what you meant, don't worry. I'll do all I can to help you find a solution.'

'I'm ready to try anything, really.'

'And you're right. There's nothing someone with your willpower can't overcome, I'm sure.'

'Thank you.'

'No, thank you. Thank you for opening my eyes to what really counts in life.'

Night hasn't fallen yet, but a golden light's already beginning to spread through the city. I feel swept away by nostalgia all of a sudden, a feeling probably brought on by the light and by all those memories, but also by this new found hope whose strength I want to absorb. Wisdom comes when you finally decide to face all those things that have caused you pain in the past. It's never too late for that.

Yes, I'm going to try and find Jonas.

8:33 pm

The car's not moving any more, but I don't feel like we've arrived yet. Suddenly Elinor's face appears at my window. I jump in surprise as joy comes over me. I open the door and hug my daughter tightly.

When I let her go, I see that Mr Kiss has already taken my suitcases out of the trunk. He's waiting for me, leaning on the car, with a business card in his hand.

'There you go,' he says.

'Thank you, Mr Kiss. How much do I owe you?'

He doesn't answer and won't let me pay him. I go back into the cab to collect my bags and all the things I left on the backseat, and glance at the meter discreetly: 119 euros, or a euro per minute I've spent in the taxi, unearthing my entire life. It's taken me twice as long to get home as it usually does, but I don't regret even a second of this trip. Time is relative, I know it now more than ever.

'Goodbye, then,' Mr Kiss says, holding out his hand for me to shake.

'Goodbye, Mr Kiss. See you soon, I hope.'

I can feel my eyes fill with tears. It's stupid, but there's nothing I can do about it.

'Are you all right, Mom?' Elinor asks. 'What's going on?'

'It's nothing, don't worry. Or rather, it's not, but I'll tell you about it later.'

Mr Kiss pulls away. I watch his car until it's no more than a grey spot I can barely make out in the distance, and then it disappears into traffic. And even then I keep looking.